A4

D0973024

4.50
Scan

Praise for **MONSTER IN A BOX**

"What a treat!"   —*New York Newsday*

"Gray is right now without peer."
                        —*The New York Times*

"Gray has become a highly polished raconteur. . . . The secret of his success is the skewed angle of vision—his eccentric wit and ruthless candor."
                        —Sylvie Drake, *Los Angeles Times*

"Spalding Gray has never been . . . more on target about his writing and performing skills. This is a star turn not to be missed."   —*Village Voice*

"Beneath a droll surface, [*Monster in a Box*] resonates with personal poignancy. Gray's performance hallmark is a laconic storytelling style in the tradition of Hal Holbrook playing Mark Twain, with a strong dose of Woody Allen thrown in . . . Thoroughly entertaining—at moments, hilarious."   —*Theater Week*

"I'd swim across continents, oceans, even to Cambodia, to spend an evening with Spalding Gray."
　　　　　—*New York Post*

"Gray is an intellectual's tale spinner. . . . [He] guides the storytelling as firmly as a practiced orchestra conductor."
　　　　　—Sheila Benson, *Los Angeles Times*

"Give him a table, a microphone, a spotlight and an audience, and this actor-author-storyteller without peer will take you on the wildest of rides through his imagination . . . one glorious experience. [Gray] does know how to refashion his life into the most exquisite art."　　　　　—*Miami Herald*

ALSO BY **Spalding Gray**

Sex and Death to the Age 14
Swimming to Cambodia

MONSTER

Spalding Gray

N A BOX

Vintage Books

A Division of Random House, Inc.

New York

A VINTAGE ORIGINAL, FIRST EDITION,
JANUARY 1992

Copyright © 1991 by Spalding Gray

All rights reserved under International and Pan-American
Copyright Conventions. Published in the United States by
Vintage Books, a division of Random House, Inc., New York, and
simultaneously in Canada by Random House of Canada Limited,
Toronto.

Library of Congress Cataloging-in-Publication Data
Gray, Spalding, 1941–
      Monster in a box / Spalding Gray.
          p.   cm.
      ISBN 0-679-73739-1
      I. Title.
    PS3557.R333M66   1992
    813'.54—dc20   91-50229
                               CIP

BOOK DESIGN BY CATHRYN S. AISON

Manufactured in the United States of America
10   9   8   7   6   5   4   3   2   1

For Renée

Acknowledgments

Monster in a Box is my thirteenth autobiographical monologue. Before opening it at Lincoln Center in November of 1990, I developed it, performing it on the road for over a year in America, Scotland, and Israel. Like my other monologues, it was not previously written down but evolved through many performances based on an outline containing key words to guide me through my stories. But, unlike my other monologues, I worked with a director, Renée Shafransky, for the first time. Working with Renée was very important for me. Her contribution as a director, editor, and co-writer was invaluable. I don't think I would have ever come to the structure of this monologue without her help. So, I'd like to thank Renée, as well as the supportive and enthusiastic audiences along the way who contributed to the birth of **Monster in a Box.**

—Spalding Gray
May 20, 1991

Preface

In March of 1990, I performed *Monster in a Box* in Washington, D.C., as a benefit for Art Against AIDS. For me, it was a very high evening, and it all went very well.

Three days after I got back to New York City, I got a phone call from a representative of the National Foundation for Mental Health. And she said, "Mr. Gray, we saw your show in Washington and we were knocked out by it. What we'd like to propose, and don't get me wrong on this, is that you become our national spokesman. I hope you don't think this is out of line with what you're doing, but we feel that we've never heard anyone so articulate about their mental illness."

MONSTER IN A BOX

Well now, I just wanted to begin by clearing up the title, so you won't spend any time thinking about what that means. This is the box. This is the Monster in it. It's a book I've been working on for the past four years, entitled *Impossible Vacation*. Due to be published by Knopf in hardcover two years ago, it's nineteen hundred pages long, and I think it's finished. There's a copy on my editor's desk, and he's beginning to cut.

When I first came to New York City to visit, just around the Christmas season of 1959, I went up to the Riverside Cathedral bell tower and looked out over New York City and made a secret pledge to myself that, when I grew up, I would move there and become a writer, inspired then by Thomas Wolfe.

I moved to New York City, but I didn't become a writer. I got involved in theater instead, and theater led to monologues, and the monologues led to publications, and the publications led to my getting a literary agent, and one day my literary agent said to me, *"I think you have a novel in you."* She sold the idea that I had one in me to Knopf, so I had to spit one up. But I didn't know how I was going to write a novel because I don't know how to make anything up, so I thought I'd write a book instead.

So I began working on this book called *Impossible Vacation.* It started out as a very simple travelogue about how whenever my girlfriend, Renée, and I try to take a vacation, I tend to . . . "complicate it" I guess would be one expression for it. "Fuck it up" might be another. I mean, I'm kind of a control freak and I like to create my own hells before the real ones get to me. I kind of like to beat hell to hell.

The book was just going to be about me, that New England puritan, who happens to find it very difficult to take pleasure when in very pleasurable places. And in the course of writing the book, I realized that the first time that I tried to take a vacation outside of the United States was when I was an actor at the Alley Theater, down in Houston, Texas, in 1967. That summer, at the end of the theater season, I went to Mexico to try to vacate and, while I was down there, my mother killed herself. And suddenly, I realized that this probably had a lot to do with why I've not been able to take a vacation very easily. And this changed the whole nature of the book, because I realized I was working with very classical themes— basically about how every boy, in order to become a man, must first in some way kill his mother off. But in my case, I think my mother and I were in competition and she beat me to it.

So the book began to grow by leaps and bounds. And I changed the names to protect the guilty. I changed the central character from my name, Spalding Gray, to Brewster North. It's still written in the first person, but it's about this guy named Brewster North who can't commit to his girlfriend Cleo—although they've been together for ten years—until he takes a vacation alone and just goes off and pleasurizes himself without complications. He just goes and learns how to hang out like a guy hanging out alone. And he wants to do this in Bali. That's where he intends to go to just hang out. He wants to go to Bali with the money that his mother left to him after she committed suicide. It wasn't a lot of money, but it had been in the bank for a long time, because it was kind of the only memorial he had to her and it had collected a lot of interest. He's taking that money out of the bank and he's going to go to Bali with it. So in a sense, I suppose you could say he's going to Bali with his mother. So the book, *Impossible Vacation,* begins in Rhode Island and it ends in Bali. That's all you need to know about the book tonight.

The monologue I'm going to perform is about something else. The monologue is about all the interruptions that happened to me while I was trying to write the book. In fact, I'd have to say the monologue you're going to hear tonight is a monologue about a man who can't write a book about a man who can't take a vacation.

Now as soon as I'd signed the contract for the book, I decided that I was going to give the monologues up. Stop doing monologues and just write. I thought the monologues were making me too extroverted. I wanted to pull back into my more introverted self and go back in and explore the private self, the shadow self, the part I hadn't been in touch with for twenty years.

I wanted to go away to a writer's colony and just write —no living, just writing. And I applied to a number of colonies, thinking that if I got accepted at a writer's colony, that would prove I was a writer and I'd be able to write. I got accepted at one of the best, the MacDowell Colony, up in Peterborough, New Hampshire, where many great writers have worked, including Thornton Wilder, who wrote *Our Town* up there and modeled Grover's Corners, New Hampshire, on the town of Peterborough. I was very excited. I went up there with great expectations.

When I got there I found six hundred acres of forest with fifty-two individual little studios or houses. I was told I'd have my own little house. And I could do anything in it I wanted, which was incredible for me, having come from New England, to return to New England and be in a house where I could do anything I wanted. It was a steamy treat. I was paralyzed there for a while. But it was a wonderful situation: they leave you completely alone in your little house, and you have no telephone so you're not bothered. You take your meals at the main house, and they bring you your lunch in a little basket, and tiptoe up and leave it on the back porch, and then tiptoe away like Yogi Bear into the forest.

Everything was fine. Everything was perfect. The only problem was the name of my house. It happened to be called "The Bates House"—named after Nurse Bates, who nursed Edward MacDowell in his final stages of syphilis. So, needless to say, I was doing all sorts of exorcisms before I got down to the writing.

Then I got down to the writing, and it was awful. I don't know why anyone would want to do it. It stinks. It's like a disease. It's an illness, writing. It steals your body from you. There's no audience. You're alone. My knuckle was swelling up. I had an arthritic knuckle from the pen pressing against it so hard while writing longhand. I was losing my sight in my left eye. I was going blind in my left eye, which was a horrible experience, because here I was working on all my Oedipal themes, and I thought, "Oh no, there goes the first eye."

So I'm writing, writing, writing, I'm writing longhand. How long can you write longhand? Three hours? Four if you're lucky, and your hand's like a claw. Then what can you do in six hundred acres of woods? You go for a walk in the woods. And you walk and you walk and you walk. You go back to the main house and you drink. And you drink and you eat. And you reread what you wrote and you get up in the morning and you write. And you walk and you walk and you drink and you eat. And you reread what you wrote and you write and you walk and you drink and you drink and you drink. And you drink. I just wanted to get out of there!

But how could I leave? I was in a privileged place. Something had to draw me away—some disaster. Someone had to have a heart attack. Who would it be?

At last what got me out of there was I received a message at the main house from the Mark Taper Forum

Theater in Los Angeles. Around the time I did the contract for the book, I also did a deal with the Mark Taper Forum Theater, never thinking it would come through. I did a deal where they were going to apply for a grant to have me in residence out there for a whole year. They were applying to the National Endowment for the Arts. That was back in the old days when the NEA was funding wild and crazy things like that.

They were going to have me in residence for a whole year, just living in L.A., hanging out, riding the buses of Los Angeles—I took it as sort of a compliment then— riding the buses of Los Angeles and finding interesting people to be interviewed on stage about living in Los Angeles. The only criterion being that these people could in no way be involved in the film industry. The project was to be called "L.A.: The Other." They call me at the MacDowell Colony and leave a message at the main house. They say the grant has come through, and I must come out. I say that's great. Now I have an excuse to leave the MacDowell Colony. I will take the Monster with me, work on it in the morning and look for "L.A.: The Other" in the afternoon.

Someone finds us a little bungalow up in the Hollywood Hills, and we move out and it is fantastic! I wake up in the morning and I discover something I had never had before—since I hadn't had it, I had never missed it—A VIEW! My God, I wake up in the morning and, there, twenty miles in the distance, a snow-capped mountain—Mount Baldy—a snow-capped mountain by a city, when you could see it the seven clear days of the year. And the sun coming over it. I mean, here in New York City, my God! I look out at a tarpaper roof on another building. At the MacDowell Colony, I looked out at a bush. But there in Los Angeles, with the sun trumpeting over Mount Baldy, we'd wake up to the smell of flowers and the sound of birds and wind chimes. And I'd get up and run over to my desk and open the Monster to work on it; the sun would stream across my writing hand and relax it. And I'd follow the sun around into the living room and have a cup of coffee, and watch the sun stream through the eucalyptus trees and have another cup of coffee, and watch the sun come through the palm trees. Then follow the sun around into the dining room, and watch the sun come through the dining room window and have a martini. Watch the sun set over Sunset Strip and have another martini. Why go out? Why bother? Why work on a book?

The only thing to get me out of there was my assistant, K.O., hired by the Mark Taper Forum. She was a redheaded freckled gal, from Southern California, taking me out to look for "L.A.: The Other." She'd drive up in her red fastback Ford. I had no idea how difficult it would be to find people not involved in the film industry until I got out there and saw a special on television—in which they were interviewing people in the parking lot of a Shop Rite supermarket. As people came out with their groceries, the interviewer would go up to them and say, "Hi there, good morning! Tell us, how's your film script going?"

And everyone said, "What! How did you know?!" Right up to the cashier.

So, K.O.'s taking me out looking. There's no way I'm going to ride the buses—they only come every four hours. Where do you look? There's no there there. Where do you begin? We're going to senior citizen centers, golden-age drop-in centers, high schools. We're driving down to Long Beach to look for Cambodian refugees. We're driving over to Venice Beach to talk with homeless living in lean-tos. We're driving downtown L.A., I'm looking down side streets. Nothing, nothing, nothing. No one.

"Wait, K.O.! I think I see some people living in a refrigerator carton down there."

She said, "Nothing going on down there, dude."

I said, "K.O., slow down will you! I know I saw something. Could you just slow down, pull over, maybe even park? And we'll walk back and hang out. Have you ever done that before? Just parked and walked?"

It was then that I realized my assistant, K.O., had what I would call a thirty-five-mile-an-hour consciousness. She simply perceived nothing on her retinas below thirty-five miles an hour. She had been on wheels since the day she was born. She started with the baby carriage, went to the roller skates, went to the skateboard, now she's in the car, and she's headed for the wheelchair. No one walks in Los Angeles—it's an old story, but I'll tell it again—no one walks in Los Angeles!

No one walked in my neighborhood—there were no sidewalks; how could they? I walked in the middle of the street dodging cars. I never saw my neighbors on their lawns. There were no children crying, no dogs barking, no televisions blaring. I mean all I heard was birds and wind chimes. It was like a neutron bomb had hit and left birds and wind chimes.

The only time I ever saw anyone in my neighborhood while walking was when I rounded the corner of the street one day and I saw some schoolbooks thrown down in the gutter with a belt around them. And then I saw the owners of the books, a Mexican-American boy and girl, high school kids, making passionate love on the side of the street. I stood over them and watched. They were French kissing. I looked down. They paid me no heed. I thought, "What better place if you want to be alone in Los Angeles?"

So I'm working on the Monster and I'm up to the section about the summer of 1965 when Brewster is desperate to get away from his mother. She's having a nervous breakdown and he's trying to help her through it, but at the same time he knows that he must get away and begin his own life or he'll never have one. He wants to become an actor. And he wants to accomplish this by getting his Equity card at the Alley Theater in Houston, Texas. He wants to go there because they are doing Chekhov's play *The Sea Gull* that season and he feels he's perfect for the role of Konstantin Gavrilovich, the young writer. He is sure that he's right for it, because he's very sensitive like Konstantin. And he has a relationship to his mother not unlike Konstantin has to his mother. Also, he likes the fact that Konstantin gets to shoot himself in the head at the end of every performance and then come back the following night to play himself again.

Brewster goes down there with great expectations that he's going to get the role. When he gets there he finds that the director has given the role to a guy who's totally wrong for it. He's not sensitive, doesn't have a mother, but has tenure. Brewster's furious about this but is unable to express his rage, because he's a New Englander. So he tries to purge himself of his anger by eating only soybeans. Soybeans morning, noon, and night. And these soybeans are causing *enormous* intestinal gas. Wherever he walks in that theater, he is leaving those silent-but-deadly, slow, hot burners. But he doesn't sit down. He just keeps moving. He's not taking responsibility for them. You see, he doesn't know how to express his anger through the proper orifice yet. Now the director of the theater senses something's wrong, and she decides to give him a better role in the next play to try to cheer him up. She gives him a better role in *The World of Sholom Aleichem*. It's a play about little Buncha Schwag and how he's so humble on earth that when he gets to heaven all the angels give him prizes and rewards. And Brewster gets to play the lead angel. And every night he's in the wings with four other angels behind him, and he's got this white angel robe that goes all the way down to the floor, with lead fish sinkers in the hem holding it down. Of course it's 1965, so he's not wearing any underwear underneath the robe, which acts as a perfect natural gas tent. Fifteen minutes' worth of slow, hot burners are building up under that robe until he makes his entrance. And he enters like a combination of Bishop Fulton J. Sheen in *Life Is Worth Living* and Loretta Young at the beginning of her television show. These magenta gas balls are pouring out from under his angel's robe and flying up in the other angels' faces. The other angels are weeping behind him!

So I'm up to that section. I'm on a roll, I'm giggling to myself as I write. It's very hot. I'm getting up and writing in my underwear. Renée is asleep naked under the bedsheets. Whoo! it's hot weather. Whoa! I sit down. That morning, not a sound. Not even the sound of birds or wind chimes. The day is frozen in heat. I sit. I can't write. It's too still and I hear—

(*rumbling sound*)

—is that thunder? Thunder in Los Angeles? No, maybe they're making a western down in the canyon. Yes, I think, they're shooting a western.

Then, all of a sudden, the strangest thing happens. I was completely unprepared for it—it was as though they were testing a hydrogen bomb in Los Alamos and set off a shock wave. I couldn't see it coming, but I felt it when it hit the house, and all of a sudden, the entire house went . . .

(*rumbling sound*)

Renée leaps up naked from under the sheets and yells, "Spald! It's the earthquake! Run for the doorjamb!"

Somewhere, Renée has read that, during an earthquake, you're supposed to stand in a doorjamb, and she's got the discipline to do it. I'm trying to get out to the front yard. I'm in my underwear running for the front door. The entire house turns to Jell-O under me! I get to the front door and Renée's jammed naked in the jamb. I can't get past her! I can't get past Renée! I'm trying to wedge under her naked body and—pop!—I'm out on the front lawn and there are all my neighbors at last, on their front lawns, dressed only in their underwear, crying, "Hi ho! Good morning! Welcome to California. You survived the earthquake, you survived the earthquake! Welcome aboard!"

Then the whole neighborhood is buzzing. There's a whole grapevine of conversation. Suddenly everyone is out there, talking. They're all talking, talking, talking about the earthquake.

"Where were you during the earthquake?"

"Oh, you're kidding!"

"He did? He was?"

"How long's it been?"

"And he thought *he* caused it? Oh lover, man, what a stud you've got there."

"That's the third one you slept through, Marge, the third one!"

"No, you can't insure those little statues." "You've got to buy canned beets, canned tuna, and distilled water to make an earthquake-kit for the big one." "Look out for 'the big one'—'the big one'!"

Then everyone stopped talking about the earthquake and went back to talking about their film scripts.

Just after the earthquake hit Los Angeles, our film, *Swimming to Cambodia,* came out. And if you haven't seen it, you should. You can rent it at your video store. It's a film of a raving, talking head—mine—talking for eighty-seven minutes about some experiences I had while playing a small role in the film *The Killing Fields.* We were very proud of it, but we didn't expect it to do that well—particularly in Los Angeles. It opened when I was out there working on my Monster and it was very popular. And all of a sudden a lot of producers wanted to get in touch with me through my agent. They all wanted to take me out to lunch to find out if I had an Idea. There are so few of them going around out there that you can get paid sixty or seventy thousand dollars if you come up with one at lunch. And I thought, all you have to do is drink enough and start talking, and something's bound to come up.

So I told Renée, "I want to take these idea lunches," and I got up to work on the Monster earlier in the morning so I could go out for the idea lunches in the afternoon. I was putting on twenty pounds from those platinum-card lunches that would begin with the bloody marys and the celery—a healthy way to drink—and go on to the sun-dried tomatoes, and the arugula mâche radicchio hot goat cheese salad, and then the poached baby salmon, the dwarf veggies, and the chardonnay, and the fumé, and the sauvignon blanc, and then the passion fruit mango mousse. And then it's time to talk ideas.

The first person to take me out was a television producer who had read a story of mine. It was a story about Renée and me driving across America and how we ran into a group of retired Americans in the Southwest who called themselves "The Good Samaritans." What they did was drive around the American Southwest in their Winnebagos, a wagon train of Winnebagos—doing good deeds. And at the end of the day, they would make a kind of wagon train circle around a campfire in a state park and sit out in their folding chairs, drinking diet sodas, and tell stories about their good deeds, kind of like

Mr. and Mrs. Lone Ranger. Renée and I were taken aboard one of the Winnebagos and given a tour, and I had written a story about it. The producer had read it and wanted to produce a TV series based on it called "The Good Sams." He said, "*You* could even play Sam."

"Well," I said, "nothing would please me more at this point in my life than to sit by a Hollywood pool and make up television situations. But I don't know how to make anything up. If I could make things up, I'd finish my book. I don't know how to tell the lie that tells the truth—I can only tell what happened to me. I'm cursed with that. But you can send me down there to the American Southwest, and I'll hang out until something happens and then call in my story on a pay phone. That's the most I can promise. But the lunch was wonderful. Thank you very much."

The next to take me out, wine me and dine me and give me a big offer, was CAA. And if you don't know what CAA is, it is the largest talent agency in the universe, I would say. It's the mafia of talent agencies. It controls the American economy. Look, I don't want to be talking about them tonight. I'd rather not, but I have to because it's part of the monologue. If they ever found out —and I'm sure they already have—that I'm talking about them, I would never work in Hollywood again. And I want to work in Hollywood again because of the health insurance. If you do three weeks' work in a feature film, you get a year's worth of major medical, dental and psychiatric. So there's no way I'm looking that gift horse in any part of its anatomy.

Now listen, when I say they've got them all, I mean it's

16

like a big club. A big power club. And they control all these package deals they put together. They've got all the big directors and all the actors. They've got them all. They've got Bob. They've got Kevin. They've got Dustin. They've got Madonna. They've got Sylvester. They've got Whoopi. They've got them all.

And I thought if they were going to sign me, that might be good for my career, because then I might have a chance to have some power in choosing the kind of role I wanted. And I pictured that I would at last be able to be cast in a kind of forthright, all-American, upstanding, heartfelt, sincere role—where I could at last get rid of my self-deprecating, New York, ironic voice. Really, I saw myself like Jimmy Stewart in a remake of *It's a Wonderful Life*—or certainly Gregory Peck in *To Kill a Mockingbird,* or maybe a new project, *Mr. Spalding Goes to Washington.* But something heartfelt, sincere, all-American, father of three. And I went in there with the intention of being really sincere and decisive.

I walked in and sat down at their big table. There's this round table, a marble table, and they were all there. About ten of them—men and women all suntanned, windblown and healthy. Oh so *healthy!* There's no more drugs in Hollywood. Health is the new drug. Those people have been up since five in the morning doing kung fu, jogging, reading scripts, and eating blue-green algae from the bottom of the Oregon lakes. I'm telling you, I walked in there and they were *ready!* I have never walked into a room and felt such a sense of *readiness* in my life. There was nothing happening, but they were *ready* for it in case it did. I walked in, and the man at the head of the table offered me the only drug left in Hollywood—a can of Diet Coke. Then he leaned in and said, "Uh, thank you very much for taking time from your busy schedule to come to meet with us. We'd all like to begin by telling you that we all hope you're not one of those artists that's afraid to make money."

And I said, "Um, how much money are we talking about?"

"Well, we did the seventeen-million-dollar Stallone deal."

"S-s-seventeen? Uh, s-s-seventeen million d-dollars, right? A-all for Sylvester?"

"That's right."

I was conflicted. I didn't know whether to say "Congratulations" or "You should be shot at sunrise." I just hoped that Sylvester had good charities he was giving to.

"And I think if you sign with us today, we could probably make you three million dollars in the next three years. In fact, we could probably start you off tomorrow as an assistant to a Ghostbuster."

And I said, "Well, that wasn't exactly what I was thinking of, but I am—I am flattered. What I'm really curious about is how did you guys find out about me?"

And he said, "We saw your film, *Swimming to Cambodia,* and I never thought I could watch anyone talk for eighty-seven minutes, particularly another man."

"What movie theater did you see it in?"

"We saw it here in the office on tape."

"But it's not out on video yet."

"We have our ways."

"Well, you could do me a favor because my father, um, my father didn't get to see it, because it showed in an art cinema in Providence, Rhode Island, and they didn't have any matinees, and he wouldn't miss cocktail hour."

Then he just reaches around and pulls what looks like a piece of plastic tubing right out from the wall, and speaking into it in a low, devilish voice, says, "Get Spalding Gray's father a copy of *Swimming to Cambodia,* will you please."

But I didn't sign. I didn't sign. I remained loyal to my old agent. I don't know why I'm loyal. I've got this loyalty thing—it's weird because I don't believe in Heaven. But I'm loyal, and the loyalty paid off. *To Kill a Mockingbird* found me in a sideways flight through my window in an odd way. The director of *To Kill a Mockingbird,* Robert Mulligan, had seen *Swimming to Cambodia,* liked it very much, and wanted to cast me in his new film, *Clara's Heart,* starring Whoopi Goldberg. He wanted me to play an ex-rabbi who had become a new-age California Jewish grief counselor. I said, "But Bob, don't you think I should be an ex-Congregational minister?"

He said, "Not at all. I grew up in Long Island and most of my Jewish friends looked Irish."

I wasn't going to argue. He cast me and I got to play the role of Dr. Peter Epstein, the new-age Jewish grief counselor. And I go around lecturing and reading from my book, *An End to Sorrow,* all the time. And I have to hold the book up and speak to groups saying things like, "Yes, if your children die, by all means mourn them. Mourn them with all your heart and soul. But not for more than seven days. And then: Enjoy!" Then I have to sign "Dr. Peter Epstein" on the back of the book and hand it out. The only problem is it has my picture on the back, which is totally confusing for me because I'm trying to write my *own* book with *my* picture on the back. They want me to sign his name on camera? I won't do it—I won't sell my soul for that price. I'm keeping the book off camera and signing *my* name across the picture and then handing it out to all the extras, pretending it's my book, finished at last.

Just after I finish shooting *Clara's Heart* I get cast in another film. I don't know what's causing this—whether it's *Swimming to Cambodia*—but I don't understand it. I get cast in *Beaches,* playing a Jewish obstetrician, with Bette Midler. I don't know where this affinity with Judaism started. Maybe back in Emerson College when I played Mr. Van Daan in *The Diary of Anne Frank.* So around about this time I was going through a kind of Hollywood conversion to Judaism. I had three weeks' work with Whoopi Goldberg and three weeks' work with Bette Midler, and it was wonderful and fun. But most important, *I got the health insurance!*

So I was able to go back to writing the Monster, feeling fully insured. I was going back to a section that took place in 1964, where the character was actually trying to get away from his mother for the first time. He had been dating her quite heavily that winter, taking her to the movies. Then winter led to summer, and he ended up swimming with her a lot in Narragansett Bay. Then after swimming they'd lie in the sun and discuss things like existentialism versus Christian Science: which is better. But he desperately wanted to get away and go to Provincetown that summer on the Cape, because everyone was down there learning how to "hang out." For the first time. Yes, that was the summer, the first in American history, that people were "hanging out." Someone had read about it and now they were doing it. You know, just leaning against a building all summer, staring out to sea with not a thought in their heads, like tanned vegetables. And Brewster wanted to get down there to try hanging out and he talks his mom into borrowing her car and he loads up the car—with her Metrecal, and Instant Breakfast, and his father's frozen meat, and his L. L. Bean sleeping bag—and he says, "Bye Mom," and drives about five miles down the road, turns around, comes back, unloads the provisions, and goes swimming with his mother. The next morning he loads the car up again. "Bye, mom!" Drives off about ten miles down the road, turns around, comes back, unloads everything. His mother never asks, "Why did you come back so soon, dear?" And they go swimming together and he doesn't make it to Provincetown that summer.

Now I'm working on that section and I get a telephone call. Someone has an idea. *They* have the idea this time, and they want to sell the idea to Columbia Pictures and send Renée and me down to Nicaragua to research a script idea for a film.

The idea was that we would join an American fact-finding team—the kind of group that had been going down there then to investigate America's illegal Contra war against the Sandinistas—and we would use this group as a study for our film script. I think these American fact-finding groups were Nicaragua's major income at that time, and the Sandinistas loved them. The script itself would be a fictional account about how once we got down there, did our thing and gave away all of our personal belongings to the Nicaraguans, our bus doesn't show up to take us to the airport. And suddenly we, or our characters, are trapped there and become very much like the people we've come to observe. I liked the idea and certainly I was interested in going to Nicaragua. It was on my list. I would much rather be actually going to Nicaragua than staying in L.A. not being able to write about not being able to go to Provincetown.

We took our idea to David Puttnam at Columbia Pictures and he said, "Great idea! Go for it!" So we did. We signed up with an American fact-finding team out of Santa Monica. They were a group of thirty-six earnest, dedicated Americans. Oh, they were so earnest that they made me feel like trash! I felt like a spy in the house of love. But I had a feeling that because of their earnestness at least the plane wouldn't crash.

We get down there and we're staying in a little ranch house that before the revolution belonged to a person and now it belonged to the people. To give you an idea of what an earnest group it was: there were doctors, teachers, lawyers, accountants. There was a pediatric dentist from Monterey who was going down there, bringing toothpaste for children. He claims he worked with children because they have puppy dog breath. "That's why your dentist suicide rate is so high in America," he said, "because of adult breath." And he's bringing boxes of toothpaste down and he tries to get these innocent cardboard boxes through passport control. But they don't believe the boxes are so innocent and they bayonet the boxes, pull it out, lick the bayonet, and say, "Oh. Okay, you may pass."

We arrive at our house, to find a swimming pool that hadn't been cleaned since the revolution, that had salad oil and black flies floating on top. You'd have to swim with your head very high above water. We went into the house, to find a radio playing Nicaraguan music. There was a big padlock around the refrigerator; the television set had *I Love Lucy* reruns on when the TV was working —kids running in from the street, watching it, loving it, loving American culture.

The house was divided into a dormitory. Renée was in with the women and I was staying with the men. I had three roommates: there was a born-again Christian from Toronto, a social worker from Ventura, and a Pedantics major from Berkeley—it was the first I'd ever heard of that one and I didn't know if he was putting me on. I tried to talk to all of them, but the born-again Christian and the social worker wouldn't talk to me. They said it wasn't revolutionary to talk about your past. But Daniel, the Pedantics major, did. I couldn't understand him though. He mumbled. He chain smoked and mumbled. Something was wrong with Daniel.

What happened was, instead of our finding the facts, the facts really began finding us. It was more like a re-education camp. They came to our house in droves. The first fact to come to our house was a Catholic nun named Mary Hartman. She'd been down there twenty-five years so she didn't have to suffer the coincidence of the sitcom. Mary Hartman was a very dedicated, very thin Marxist Catholic nun who demanded food for the people *now*. No pie in the sky by and by, if you please! She reminded me of Celia Coplestone in T.S. Eliot's *The Cocktail Party,* who, when she finally got disillusioned with romantic love and was looking for a larger love, went to a therapist and said:

> I should really *like* to think there's something wrong with me—
> Because, if there isn't, then there's something wrong,
> Or at least, very different from what it seemed to be,
> With the world itself—and that's much more frightening!
> That would be terrible. So I'd rather believe
> There is something wrong with me, that could be put right.

And Celia ends up going to South America to become a missionary and gets crucified on an anthill.

Then an economist came to the house and I was starting to get cross-eyed, trying to listen to all the facts. He's got an American accent—or, I don't know, maybe he's an American speaking with a Spanish accent. I can't figure him out. He's lecturing to us, saying things like "Nicaragua is not a pure communist economy. It's a mixed economy. It is not a Russian satellite. It has many countries that are giving it support. America spends more money on shaving cream every year than the entire Nicaraguan economy." Then he tells us how the CIA comes down there and ruins the economy by starting things like toilet paper rumors, by saying there will soon be a shortage of toilet paper. So of course everyone rushes out and buys up all the toilet paper. They hoard it and there is a shortage. And he says, "Do you know how long it takes to rebuild the people's confidence in a thing like toilet paper?" Then he raises his fist at the end and passionately cries, "Don't we have a right to wipe?!"

And then there were farmers, and teachers, and doctors. We went to visit a hospital and after a while it was all like a Dick and Jane primer, you know. Like, "See Carlos bleed. Hear Juan cry." I couldn't take it all in! I mean I was all "fact up." I just wanted to collapse into a nonfactual situation.

Finally, we were taken up to Matagalpa. We didn't know what facts we were going to be exposed to—but we were given a very big meal like the one they give you just before you go to the electric chair. We were the only ones in the restaurant at noon. It was a hundred ten degrees out. Up until then, we'd been eating rice and beans every day. Suddenly, we were having steak, rice, and beans, and Nicaraguan beer, which was wonderful. I was sitting across from my roommate Daniel—he was not eating, which was probably wise considering the heat —and I was taking little slices of his meat and sipping his beer.

After lunch we were taken up to a shed with a tin roof and a dirt floor and it was very hot. We had no idea what facts we were going to be exposed to. Then in came the mothers of the heroes and the martyrs. There were about twenty-five of them—and I have to describe them as something like a combination of an A.A. meeting and a very perverse performance art piece, because they have been testifying, innumerable times, about the horrors that have been inflicted on their loved ones. And, as far as I'm concerned, they don't have to speak anymore. There is an aura of grief that is coming off of them that is so strong that we could just sit there and meditate on that and get the message. But they do speak and they begin their testimonial. They say:

"My son, his name was Oscar. They threw him from a helicopter. I never found his body. He was sixteen."

"My daughter was Rosa. They cut off her breasts, her arms, her legs. I never found all of her. She was thirteen."

"They put a metal rod through my son's head. It went through one ear and out the other. Please go tell your President Reagan to stop these horrors. Please!"

Never did they mention the fact that the CIA was trained with our tax dollars to teach the Contras how to put metal rods through people's heads. No, they just said, "Go tell your President to *please* stop these horrors." They had this wonderful naive idea that we could go directly to the White House, because Daniel Ortega lived around the corner from all of them, in a ranch house. And he was completely approachable in that little country the size of the state of Illinois.

Because of the heat and the beer and what they're saying I can barely stay awake. Also I am feeling guilty for being down there for Columbia Pictures. I'm just sitting there nodding out and trying to picture myself with a blow-dried hairdo and dressed in a Palm Beach suit walking up the steps of the White House to speak to President Reagan about stopping those horrors. And I can't stay awake, and I'm feeling guilty about that as well. And I look around and see that no one else in the group seems able to stay awake. But they all have their tape recorders going so they're getting every bit of it. The only person who's not nodding out in our group is Daniel, my Pedantics roommate, and he is *wired*! I have never seen anyone listen so intensely. He is listening with such energy that I stay awake by watching him listen. Then at the end of their testimony the mothers file out and Daniel gets up and comes right across to me, like a magnet, and says, "Come here!"

I say, "What?"

"Tell me, was I . . . was I just put on trial just then for being a counterrevolutionary?"

I say, "Daniel, that had nothing to do with you as far as I know. They never mentioned your name once."

"No. No, I want to know the truth. Are you here—are you here—are you here to . . . help me or to report on me?"

Is this man reading my mind? I wonder. Does he know I'm a spy for Columbia Pictures? "What are you talking about?" I ask.

"CIA is what I'm talking about!" Daniel says. "They're in our group and I know you're one."

Why do these people always choose me? I wonder. This happens often. Out of the whole group—is there some meaning in this? I say, "Daniel, I'm not CIA. I can't be. I don't know how to make anything up. If I could make things up, I'd finish my book."

He says, "No, no, they're here. There are six of them—they're following me. They're in the group. They're speaking through my teeth, they're spraying my food—that's why I'm not eating, they're spraying my food!"

I say, "Wait. Group leader! Group Leader, could you come in here please!"

And Daniel cries, "No! No! She's the leader. She's a CIA leader!"

He flips out. He starts moaning and groaning and tearing at his hair. And the entire group comes in and gathers around him like a great doughnut, like a life preserver, to keep him from being put in a Nicaraguan insane asylum. All the way back to the house, we're around him while he is bouncing in the middle and tearing at his hair. Then, everyone has to take care of him. Everyone has to take a shift with him. Some people, thinking it's hypoglycemia, are trying to force-feed him like a goose.

Then my turn comes to take care of him and I find I'm the least able to deal with him, which is really weird for me because, up until the time I went to Nicaragua—because of the guilt I was feeling for my mom—I was seriously thinking that I should give up show business and become a psychiatric social worker. This man cured me of that fantasy. If nothing else happened to me in Nicaragua, he cured me of that fantasy. I mean I think I have a big boundary problem and it felt like his insanity was leaking into mine.

So I put on this stern voice and said, "No, Daniel. No, Daniel, no. You come over here and eat. No, there's no CIA in our group. There is no CIA in our group. . . . I don't *think* . . . No, eat your food. No, shut up, Daniel. No, you're crazy!"

Finally, it turned out that we had a psychiatric social worker in our group, and she took him aside and said, "Daniel, tell me, what was it you were taking in the United States that you did not bring with you here?"

Trying to get him out of Nicaragua was a real trial. He tried to eat his passport while going through passport control. We got him out of the country, thank goodness, and we got him back to Los Angeles Airport. A stretch limo picked him up at LAX. I hoped his mother was in it. I hoped he was going for a long rest. Renée and I didn't stick around to find out.

Back at the house I was pacing around saying, "Renée, Renée, what are we going to do? What are we going to write about? I didn't see anything in Nicaragua. I couldn't even tell you where we were. All I saw was the inside of one psychotic pedantic American's mind. What shall we do?"

She said, "Spald, calm down, we'll make something up."

I said, "I don't know how to make anything up, Renée. I would finish my book if I could make things up!"

She said, "Well, *I'm* going to make something up. You go do what you have to do."

So I go in to open the Monster to see if I'd gotten any distance on it over the fourteen days. I sit down, I open it. I'm in my undershirt. I can't concentrate. It's ninety-two degrees in November! I'm thinking, "When is the endless sunshine going to stop? When will my body be covered in wool and corduroy so I can think again?"

I look over at the answering machine. It's on overblink with all the messages that have piled up since we've been in Nicaragua. I push the Monster aside and go to take the messages off the machine.

The first message to come off the machine is from HBO. They want me to do a new HBO special in which I travel around the United States interviewing people who have just been taken aboard flying saucers. And I call them back and say, "Oh yeah! No, no it's not an insult at all. You've come to the right person. It's right up my alley. No no, I'm sure they're out there. . . . No. But I'll tell you what . . . No, I can't talk now but—I'll be down soon to talk about the details."

The next message I take off the answering machine is from an independent filmmaker from India. And he's had an epiphany. He's seen the poster for *Swimming to Cambodia*. If you haven't seen it, it's a very distressed head—my head—floating in water and it's either just surfacing from the water or about to go down for the last time, depending on how you look at it. He has seen the poster and here's how he looks at it: He's had an epiphany that he must bring me to India, to the Kumbamaila, which is a religious festival that happens every seven years where the three holy rivers, the Jhelum, the Saraswarti, and the Ganges come together in a great maelstrom. And two million people gather on the edge of it and start hurling themselves in. Those that are holy pop up like corks; those that aren't—under and drowned. Seven years ago, two thousand people drowned. Two thousand! And he wants to take me there, throw me in, and film my reaction. This is the only call that Renée

30

intercedes on. I hear her from the other room yelling, "Spald, do not return that phone call!"

And I'm pacing. I'm pacing around the table. I'm frantic from all the things I feel I must do. The mothers of the heroes and the martyrs are still in my head—*"Go tell President Reagan!"* L.A.: The Other! "K.O.! I'll be right out. Just drive around the block, I'll be right out. My agent's on the phone"—with the book and the Monster—got to finish the Monster, get the character back from Provincetown, and Thanksgiving is coming. Thanksgiving's coming! Thanksgiving's coming and Renée is saying, "Please, Spald, can't we go back East for Thanksgiving? We won't recognize it out here. Please? I want to see my friends."

"All right, all right, Renée. We'll take a five-day excursion. Just put everything aside for five days. And we'll just do that, and that's the last interruption."

So we get a cheap five-day excursion ticket. The day we're supposed to fly, I'm in the bathroom brushing my teeth and I hear Renée cry out, "Spald!"

I say, "What, Renée? What is it?"

"I have a spider bite on my thigh! It's a big spider bite!"

I say, "Renée, what would a spider be doing in bed with you in November? Here, put some calamine lotion on it—we're supposed to fly today. Just put a whole pile on."

We get to New York and Renée spends the entire Thanksgiving day lifting her skirt, showing her friends her spider bite. It has now turned into blue shingles, I mean, bright, fluorescent blue shingles creeping up her leg. I'm in bed with the covers over my head. I don't like the looks of it—it frightens me and I don't know why.

The day after Thanksgiving—we have one day before we're supposed to fly back—I have all these invitations to screenings of films. Because of *Swimming to Cambodia,* I've received all these invites. We have one to go see Cher's new film, *Moonstruck,* at the Museum of Modern Art, and I think, well goodness, why not? It's free. I'll give it a try. And so I tell Renée to meet me there.

I arrive on time; Renée arrives early. It's cold. She goes across the street to the public library to warm up, and she comes out, and she's coming toward me. And she's got that face. Oohhhhh, that face! Something's wrong. Someone's dying or she's read a letter of mine she shouldn't have read. She comes over, she puts her hand on my forehead and says, "Spald, do you have a fever?"

I say, "I don't have a fever, Renée. Come on, spit it out, what happened?"

And Renée says, "I just went in the library to warm up and there was this book that was open like it was waiting for me. It was open to color photos of all the rashes that you get when you have AIDS. And mine was there!"

I just went, "Oh! Uh . . . Oh! What library? Um, Renée . . . You're Renée, right? I'm Spalding. Um, wait a minute. Um." (Denial.) "Uh wait! Now why did we come to New York City for Thanksgiving? What was that—whose idea was that?" (Denial.) And my feet began to sweat. I've never wanted to disappear from a place more in my life. My feet were sweating so much I was leaving sponge marks on the sidewalk in front of the museum. My mouth went dry. So dry. I couldn't spit if I wanted to. And every time I tried to deny what was going on at that moment, I would start barking. I was barking like a dog in front of the Museum of Modern Art. I was pacing and barking and leaving these sponge marks on the sidewalk.

Renée said, "Spald, calm down. Calm down. Let's go see *Moonstruck* and try to forget about it for a bit." And remember, it was she who had the rash.

I said, "Renée, what are you talking about?"

She can lose herself in the movies, just walk right in and disappear. So we go in to try to forget about it for a little bit, and I'm sitting, trying to get into the movie, but every time I see Cher, I don't see Cher. I see instead the face of that sleazy, sexy, stage-door-Judy—with the very questionable sex and drug habits—that I went home with one night after a show. A long time ago. *But not long enough ago!* And every time I see that face I start barking like a dog.

And Renée says, "Spald, stop it! Do you realize you're barking inside the Museum of Modern Art?! Stop it! People are staring at you. In fact, Cher is staring at you!"

I turn around and there is Cher. I can't believe that she's surrounded by an entourage of men with orange and purple hair—and she's staring at *me?* I go back, I try to watch the screen, but every time Cher is on screen, I see that sleazy, sexy Judy's face instead. And now I'm growling. I'm growling in the Museum of Modern Art!

And Renée says, "Spald, stop it. Now we're going to have to leave. MacNeil Lehrer is behind you taking notes."

I turn around and there he is—I don't know which one—but he's there! And he's taking notes. And what's amazing is that every time I notice a celebrity looking at me, and I'm in their gaze, I'm not afraid of death or dying. (I haven't been able to analyze that one yet.)

We get back to Los Angeles and the spider bite, or whatever it is, is gone. It's just pretty much disappeared. But the whole situation has triggered in me this irrational, off-the-wall, out-of-control AIDS hysteria. I am now convinced that I am carrying the virus and that I'm about to explode at any minute like a disease bomb. And let me tell you, National Public Radio was not helping one bit that winter. Every night at five, *All Things Considered* was reporting the latest risk groups. "High-risk" for AIDS was out. "Risk" was in, that winter. And you would be amazed how many of us fit into that category. I certainly did, and the Christian Scientist in me was saying, "Simply don't turn the radio on at five"—it's better not to, because in Christian Science, to name the disease is to get it, to absolutely get it—while the Freudian in me was saying, "Turn it on, because to name it is to claim it. To name it is to take away its power." So the Freudian in me was turning the radio on and the Christian Scientist in me was turning it off. Freud: on. Christian Science: off. On: "Uncircumcised males"—off. On: "Fifty percent chance"—off. On: "HIV-positive female ..." I'm pacing around the table, my feet are sweating, my mouth is dry, I'm barking like a dog. And I'm sitting there trying to write my book and I'm at a very difficult point. It's that summer of 1965, and I'm at home with my mother, trying to help her through her nervous breakdown by reading to her from Alan Watts's book *Psychotherapy East and West,* laboring under that romantic R.D. Laing idea that was so popular then that everyone who has a nervous breakdown is so lucky, because they get to come out at the other side with such great wisdom—provided they get through to the other side. And I was there reading from Alan Watts, trying to help my mom through to the other side. But she wasn't listening. She was reading from Mary Baker Eddy's *Science and Health,* and from *The Christian Science Monitor.* And I remember that day: she, curled up on the couch, a warm July day. And she had *The Christian Science Monitor* between us, like a Japanese paper wall. And I got so annoyed at not being able to get through, I just reached down and popped the paper with my finger.

And she pulled the paper down and looked me right in the eyes and said, "How shall I do it, dear? How shall I do it? Shall I do it in the garage with the car?"

And I'm sitting at the desk and I can't write. I'm sitting there sweating and the California sun is streaming in on my arm illuminating every imperfection. And I'm saying, "Renée, bring the magnifying glass! It's not a freckle. Look, look at this. It's a blue spot! Come over here and look at it! Look at the back of my tongue— what is that? Is it white there? Look at my cheekbones! I didn't have cheekbones like this yesterday! Am I losing weight?"

She said, "Spald, I can't deal with it. I simply can't

write the script. I can't write the Nicaragua script and nurse you at the same time. You've either got to go get tested or shut up."

I said, "Renée, I don't want to get tested for AIDS. I don't want to know when I'm going to die."

Then she said, "All right. If you don't want to get tested for AIDS, then let's deal with the flying saucers. You've taken on too much, you're on overload. You've got to make your priorities. Let's make a list. Do you want to do the HBO flying saucer project or not?"

All right, we decide to research the HBO UFO project, and this takes my mind off death and dying, for a while. We go down to the Hollywood flatlands to a group called Skywatch, which is a kind of support group for people who have recently been taken aboard flying saucers, and they are speaking for the first time about this experience. And we go down to this little bungalow in the Hollywood flatlands. We come in and find a seat. There are about thirty people there, all crowded in and sitting on folding chairs. There's a cozy fire in the fireplace, and about six people are sitting up at the end of the room where they are going to testify for the first time about their experience.

And let me tell you, in my opinion, those extraterrestrials are not imparting any great wisdom to these people. Basically, they are harassing them. They are making fuzzy minds fuzzier. They're cutting behind their ears. They're giving them anal probes. I mean, one man stood up, very depressed, and said, "I'm from La Jolla and I used to watch a lot of TV before I was taken aboard the ship. Now I don't. Now I just watch these little dots come through the keyhole of my living room door and make crazy hazy patterns in the room."

At this point, Renée just turned to me and said, "Spald, let's get out of here before what happened to them happens to us."

Cross that off the list. Alienate HBO. And Christmas is coming! Christmas is coming! And the only reason I knew Christmas was coming was because I heard it on the radio. I never would have noticed it out there. And this Christmas, all I can hear is that line going over and over in my head: "All the world's a hospital, and either you're a patient or you're a nurse." And I did not want to be a patient again that Christmas. I wanted to help people needier than I. I thought that's what the problem was—why I was so hypochondriacal—I was surrounding myself with myself too much, I was being too narcissistic. Put it aside, help others, help needier people.

Keeping with the theme of suicide, I decided that Christmas to apply to the Los Angeles suicide hotline and answer suicide calls for Christmas. I thought, "Wouldn't it be better to actually prevent a suicide than not be able to write about not being able to prevent one?" So I sent for an application. It was six pages long. And I filled it out—I was amazed how long it was—and then I went down for a two-hour interview. Two people were interviewing me. In the course of it they said something about how I might, in order to learn how to answer these calls, have to go to school for six weeks. And when I heard that, I said, "School? Oh no! But I wanted to answer suicide calls for Christmas!"

"Mr. Gray, my colleague and I found it very interesting talking with you, but we both agree that it would be wise for you to go into therapy and to come back and work with us in a year's time."

I go out of there. My feet are sweating worse than ever, my mouth is dry, and I'm barking. I mean, when the suicide hotline tells you to go into therapy, it's time!

So I do it. I do what they advise me to do. I begin my earnest search for a therapist.

The first guy that I go to wants to charge me $126 a session. He's a psychiatrist, and he wants to prescribe drugs, medicine—I don't know what—mood elevators. I'm not interested in drugs. I pay him a $126 check. And leave.

The next therapist I go to is a woman who was highly recommended to me. She was supposed to be very smart and to work very fast. I get there. In the course of the therapy, the AIDS hysteria comes up and she says, "Look, I think if you've not been monogamous for the past seven years, chances are you've come in contact with the virus. And what I'd like you to do is go home and live your life for the week with that knowledge and then come in and we'll see where we go from there." And I wrote her an eighty-dollar check. And all the time I was writing the check, I wanted to fall on her and strangle her.

I get back. I'm pacing. My feet are sweating. Renée says, "What's going on? You should feel better after you've come back from a therapist. This woman's got to be reported. I'm calling the therapy police."

Next, I decide I must go to a Jungian. Why? Because

38

I'm not experiencing the shadow anymore—the Jungian shadow. I'm not in touch with it. Why? Because there are no shadows in L.A. That damn sun is wiping them all away. So I decide to go to the Jung Institute and I have this man recommended to me named Dr. Alfred Traummamen. And I think, "Spalding, what's in a name? Why even bother to go driving down there?" But I did. And I arrived and looked down at the floor as he opened the door, and I saw loafers with gold bars, green gabardine pants, matching gabardine shirt, blow-dried Beatle haircut, mustache. We go in and sit down, and he begins lecturing to me about the Jungian shadow and how we have to explore the shadow in us. He begins reading to me from Jung's notebooks and from his own notebooks. And I'm thinking, "How am I going to get out of here before the hour's up? How? Shall I just walk out?" I stayed for the whole hour and at the end, left without paying him anything.

By now I'm hysterical and desperate. I come back to the house saying, "Renée, they told me I should find a therapist. I don't know what to do. They're probably right, but I have to interview the L.A. people. I don't have time to find a good therapist. I'd have to look at so many—and the Monster and—K.O.'s outside—and the mothers of the heroes and the martyrs want me to go tell President Reagan—!"

Renée said, "Spald, please calm down, I think you should do the interviews. And what I would do is, as you're interviewing the people, simply ask them if they know of any good therapists in the Los Angeles area."

So I begin the interviews at the Mark Taper. I've

found forty people that I assume aren't involved in the film industry. I'm interviewing four people a night and I work about a half an hour with each person.

The first person who comes up claims he's a "walk-in." He weighs 325 pounds. He claims he's so fat because he has a small extraterrestrial that's "walked into" him and is living inside of him. The E.T. is very vulnerable, so that's why he's so fat, because he has to protect the little creature within him. And he does workshops in which he drives up and down the California coast, and this little extraterrestrial speaks through him. And then after the workshops, he goes out to Denny's and orders fifteen milkshakes to stay fat.

Next I interviewed three valley girls. They came on stage together. They were wonderful. I asked them if they had any religious practices and they said the only religious practice they had was called "Sweet Sixteen."

And I said, "What's that?"

They said when they reach sixteen, they stand on the lawn, and all their friends stand in a circle and watch their parents give them a new car.

Then I interviewed Raymond, a wonderful ninety-eight-year-old Japanese man who lived in Skid Row. He'd lived in the same neighborhood since 1904, in this one-room little place in downtown L.A. Now he goes to Santa Anita every day to play the horses.

The next person I interviewed was Charles Manson's lawyer. He's given up on people since Charlie, and now he only handles cases where there are large thefts. By that I mean, like, a piece of a freeway, a house, a Goodyear blimp, a cement mixer, something big that's stolen.

Then the ultimate Los Angeles story. I interviewed a woman who had just been picked up by a spaceship. By the way, during all these interviews, I was never judgmental. I was like an open conduit. I was not like Donahue, Morton Downey, Jr., or Geraldo. I was able to suspend the window of disbelief for about two hours until I got home and opened the beers—and then the judgment flowed! Anyway, this woman's story was this: just last August, she had been taken aboard a mother spaceship on the Ventura Spaceway—uh, Freeway. Her entire van was picked up. She was given a tour of the spaceship. They zapped her to make her lose her memory. She only realized that she had been picked up because she was headed the wrong way on the freeway. She was driving west on the freeway and an hour later, she was driving east. And she'd lost an hour from her life, and she wanted it back. So she had to be hypnotized, digressed, regressed, and she had total recall of the mother ship picking her van up, holding it and being given a full tour of the ship. She was shown the terrarium, the solar panels and also described the little E.T. faces in full detail.

And then the next night I interviewed a man who runs the Aetherius Society. The Aetherius Society is a small group that's located in Los Angeles and London—interesting juxtaposition. What they believe is that all the great avatars—Mohammed, Krishna, Buddha, Jesus—have gone to different planets in the solar system and are sending back flying saucers that circle the earth fifteen thousand miles up. And these flying saucers are sending down positive energy that the Aetherius Society stores in a big battery. I went to their service and the battery looks very much like one of those electric radiators on stilts. Everyone holds hands around the battery and prays while the energy flows in. Then, when there's a disaster in the world, they take the battery to a granite mountain—it has to be granite—Mount Adams in the White Mountains, Mount Shasta in California. And they all gather around it and aim that energy at the natural disaster. The Mexico City earthquake was the last one they focused on. Only, for some reason, they only aim it at the relief workers—not the victims—and they zap those workers with positive energy.

And I said, "Really? Well, that's fascinating. Have any of your people ever been picked up by a flying saucer?"

"Oh no no no," he said. "That could never happen. They're fifteen thousand miles up."

I said, "Really? Because we had a woman in here yesterday who was picked up by a mother spaceship on the Ventura Freeway."

And he just turned to me, rolled his eyes, made a screwy cuckoo sign with his finger, and said, "Well, it takes all kinds."

Finally after two weeks of interviews, I have a waitress come up. She's been a waitress for twenty-three years at the Cantor's Deli in the Fairfax area. She comes up. And halfway through the interview, she takes out her film script and dumps it in my lap. It's about two killer whales that are in love with each other. One of them is trapped in Marineland, the other's out in the Pacific Ocean. And they have a little eight-year-old girl as a go-between, trying to get them back together again. I stagger off that stage going, "Whoa! Thank God, thank God! It's over. Cross that one off the list."

I didn't find a therapist, but I completed the project. And I went and collapsed in front of my dressing room mirror and I thought, now that's interesting. I haven't thought about death or dying for two weeks. Isn't it therapeutic to surround yourself with people weirder than yourself! And no sooner did I think that, than my feet started sweating, my mouth went dry. I saw my skull in the mirror, I saw the white spots on my tongue and I . . . at the same time I heard this knock knock knocking on my dressing room door and I got up to open it and my savior came through the door with his card, this tall, smiling man, and the card read "Dr. Peter Lamston. Psychoanalysis."

I said, "Psychoanalysis? Oh my God, I'm not ready for that. I don't think I have time for that."

And he said, "Believe me, Spalding, I think you do. I think your subconscious is so close to the surface I can see its periscope."

Immediately I liked this man. First of all, he's doing psychoanalysis. Psychoanalysis in L.A. in this day and age? Everyone's doing primal scream and birthing and getting it over with in a weekend. And he's doing the old slow talking cure. All right, I think, I will give him a try, and just go one time to talk with him. So I go for one consultation. In Century City.

I like his office very much. It's on the twenty-fourth floor of a skyscraper. The only skyscrapers in L.A. are in Century City. Very Freudian, very New York. But in order to get there—in order to get to the twenty-fourth floor—you have to drive under Century City, deep down into the underground parking lot. Down, down, down. Earthquake, earthquake, earthquake. Park the car. Run, run, run to the elevator. Up, up, up and "pop" you're out. And then you have to get your parking ticket validated so you can park for free. You have to purchase something in the mall: I got a haircut. And afterward I got my parking ticket validated.

I go up to Dr. Peter's twenty-fourth-floor office and I go in. And immediately I like him. He's happy. I know that I can't upset him no matter what I say—he's a happy man.

The other thing that I like is that his office is divided in the most interesting way. Over on the left side is the Freudian section: a couch, two leather chairs, three boxes of pink Kleenex. Then, dividing the office there is a huge tropical fish tank with everything in it: the fighting fish, the pearl gouramis, the angelfish, bubbles coming out of the divers—you could free-associate on those for hours. And then on the other side of this tropical fish tank is what looks like a children's playground. Well, I don't know, I assume it's for children—I'm certainly gravitating toward it. There's a little sandbox, a little low table, an easel, and toys. So we begin working in the Freudian side and he asks me, "What's the problem?"

And I say, "Well, every time I sit down to try to finish my book, I feel like I'm dying, particularly of AIDS."

"Really? What are your symptoms?"

"Well, my feet are sweating in a big way. I change my socks three, four times a day. My mouth is dry, I couldn't

44

spit now if you asked me to. And well, I'm uh, I'm . . . uh
. . . barking."

"Well I really don't think we could call those
symptoms, Spalding. What I'd like to find out is what's
going on in that book you're trying to write. Could you
tell me about that? I think your problems have to do with
what's in that book. Would you tell me the story of that?"

Well, I begin to tell him and we realize it's such a long
story it's going to take three sessions a week. And I agree
to come—classical psychoanalysis, three sessions a week.
And he gives me a good deal. He reduces the price and,
don't forget, I've got the health insurance. So at the end
of the first session I take out a check to pay him but I
don't have a pen. Here I'm a writer without a pen, he's a
psychoanalyst without a pen. So he takes me over to the
children's section, and he sits me down at the little kids'
table. And then he comes over with a box of crayons and
says, "Choose your color."

I choose a magenta crayon to sign my check with. I'm
signing away, looking up at him towering over me, and
I'm thinking, *This is the right relationship.*

So I'm coming to him three times a week. And I'm
driving down, down, down, parking, and coming up, up,
up. I can't get a haircut three days a week—it doesn't
grow in fast enough—so I've got to get my ticket
validated by going and buying the cheapest thing I can
find. I go to a stationery store and I buy a Pilot pen for
ninety-nine cents. But I immediately put the Pilot pen in
my Danish schoolbag, because I like signing my checks so
much with different colored crayons.

Now we're working very fast and very hard, and I'm

telling him the story of my book. Certainly I know what the cure in psychoanalysis is supposed to be, so I'm looking both ways. I don't want it to take me by surprise because I'm not really sure that I want the cure. I know the cure is supposed to be the transformation of hysterical misery into common unhappiness. And God knows I have a lot of hysterical misery, but I'm not sure I want to let go of it.

Now in the course of trying to let go of the hysterical misery, I get an invitation, I get an offer. I get something outside of therapy that gives me such a sense of self-esteem that it almost cures me. It stops my feet from sweating. I get an offer to take my film, *Swimming to Cambodia,* to the first American film festival in Russia. And I cannot believe this. I don't know how they found me or why they want me, but they've invited the following films: *Hoosiers, Rumblefish, Cool Hand Luke, Children of a Lesser God, The Empire Strikes Back, An Officer and a Gentleman, The Wizard of Oz, Splash!,* and *Swimming to Cambodia.* Wow, I think, what an honor. I really want to go, but I'm frightened. I don't want to end up in a Russian insane asylum. The last thing I want to do is start barking in the streets of Moscow. So I think I'll go to Dr. Peter and talk with him about it. And if he feels I'm in good enough shape to go, I'll go.

And Dr. Peter says, "Spalding, I think things are going very well with you. I think this is a wonderful, wonderful invitation. You seem much better. Your feet have dried up, and you're able to relate to me now in a non-performance mode. But I think you should be careful, because Russia is a very depressing place. Particularly now in February. The sun never shines."

I said, "Great! I'm going!"

We arrive in Moscow and we're staying in the Sovyetskaya Hotel with the great marble columns and the red carpets—it's like *Eloise Goes to Moscow*! I'm up in bed in my Chinese long silk underwear, snuggling with six wool blankets piled on top of me, snuggling like a kid bunking school. I jump up out of bed. I run to the window and open the curtains and open the blinds and open the shutters and look out. Renée says, "What do you see, hon?"

I go, "Nothing! Nothing! Nothing! It's like a Beckett play! NOTHING!" All I see is gray-white snow coming down to meet gray-white snow. On the horizon, Russians scurry by like little furballs.

We turn on the TV to watch Russian morning news. It's called *120 Minutes*. Basically, what it is is two Russians, a man and a woman, reading from that morning's newspaper. You can hear the newspaper pages rustle on the microphone and you see the camera do close-ups of paragraphs.

Then it's time to go down for breakfast. And it's old food. Oh! The food is old. It's old eggs cooked thirty seconds, and coffee with no caffeine—I don't mean decaf —I mean NO caffeine, I mean NYET caffeine, NYET! It's all been removed for hospitals for medicinal purposes only. Now Renée and I were told about that before we came over. So we brought a pound of Nicaraguan coffee with us. And, not being socialists, we were brewing it up

47

in our room, alone. We were the only ones in our entire group to come down *awake*. "Hi! Good morning! We love Russia!" All the other actors were coming down with their sleep masks on their foreheads going, "Coffee, coffee, just what the doctor ordered! No, it looks black, looks nice and all. Is that Turkish coffee? I don't know why it doesn't wake me up! It looks like Turkish coffee. I don't know what's going on here. I don't know why I can't get a buzz. I don't know why I can't take a shit."

Then, after breakfast, there is a tour bus waiting outside and everyone has to vote as to where they want to go on a group tour that day. Oh, you might have a choice of a fort, or a church, a tomb, or a museum, or to go buy lacquer boxes at the American dollar shop, or go see the pickled babies, depending on what your mood is.

Now if you don't want to go on a group tour, you're relatively free to just go off on your own in a taxi, provided you can get a taxi to stop. I mean, why should they stop? They get paid to drive around alone all day. We were told that the only way to get them to stop was to hold up a crush-proof pack of Marlboros. You hold it up; it's the only color in Moscow in February. You've got the red stars on the Kremlin and you've got the Marlboro boxes. They never plow the roads, it's all white. And the cabs don't have any snow tires. So we hold it up, they see the box, the cab comes to a slow sliding stop and Renée runs over.

Renée speaks enough Russian to tell them we don't want to pollute their lungs. We only have one pack of Marlboros and we'd rather not open it. Is there anything else besides cigarettes they would like from us?

48

And to our surprise they reply in English, "Yes, if you have any. Pilot pens." And of course I had a whole Danish schoolbag just filled with them. I was handing them out, and we were getting cabs all over Moscow.

Now, the first thing that I find disappointing in Moscow is that there is no vodka. I don't see any vodka. I'm looking everywhere. Prohibition's going on, but you wouldn't know it. No one's talking about prohibition. There's just no vodka. You go into a bar—you go into the hottest writers' club or actors' club—and all the writers and actors are there, drinking Diet Pepsi and eating old lox. They're passionate. No one's saying "Do you remember the vodka?" or "When will the vodka come again?" There's just no mention of it. But they're still passionate. I always thought the vodka caused the Russians to be passionate. No, not at all; with them it's genetic. The vodka causes *me* to be passionate. And I wanted it. So I call my translator, Misha, over. "Misha, come over here, please." Misha looks like a demented version of Robin Williams in *Moscow on the Hudson*. I say, "Misha, look, tell me, why is there no vodka in Moscow?"

Misha just throws up his arms and says, "One day . . . no vodka!"

I wanted to buy a bottle of vodka so I could fill up my little Smirnoff bottles that I was carrying with me. They had started out full and now they were empty. For years I had been carrying them around with me, pouring drinks under the table in order to save money. I have been pouring drinks under the table since 1967 and never gotten caught. I've been pouring drinks under the table from the highest to the lowest, from the Rainbow Room to Burger King and never gotten caught. In fact I saved enough money from pouring drinks under the table to buy a SoHo loft.

I don't do it anymore, I've given up on it. But here's how I used to do it—I'll tell you in case you should ever want to do it. First of all, don't buy the little bottles. Get them from American Airlines, or whatever airline you fly, for free. Then go out and buy a plastic half gallon of Popov vodka for $11.99. Don't spend money on vodka. Now in my opinion, there is no difference between Popov and Stolichnaya. Whenever my friends tell me that, I do a blindfold test and they lose. In fact, I take empty bottles of Absolut, fill them with Popov and put them in my freezer. My guests love it! So, get your Popov. Then go buy a white plastic funnel at Woolworth's for fifty-nine cents. Line your bottles up in the morning and fill them up—gals, you can put four of these in your pocketbook; guys, you can put two in either jacket pocket. And you're off for your busy day and to your fancy restaurant at night. When you get to the restaurant what do you get first? A big glass of ice water. So you have a great setup. You just drink the water down, and you're left with your ice, and you're all set to go with the vodka—provided that is, you can keep the water boy away from the table. "No! No more water! No, just leave the ice. I'm going to be working with it throughout the evening." When you get rid of the water boy, then you get the bottle out under the table. And then—here's the hard part—you have to make something up. In order to distract the waiter. You have to pretend that you are having a passionate conversation with the person across from you. It's hard for me to make things up but I'd try pretending to talk about, oh, a film deal or an affair. Then as you're leaning in passionately talking, you just pour the bottle into your glass under the table.

So I said, "Renée, please, I'm desperate. Call down to room service for some vodka."

And Renée said, "Spald, there's no room service in Russia."

"Well, call the kitchen. Call somewhere."

So Renée calls the kitchen and she speaks enough Russian to get a one-pint bottle of Russian vodka sent up —for sixty American dollars. I fill my bottles and I'm off to the opening-night ceremonies.

When we arrive for the opening night ceremony of the film festival, the first thing we see is all these Russians dressed like peasants singing around us with tambourines, and they begin herding us like lost sheep into the auditorium. We are herded up on stage. Looking out, all we can see is this ocean of fur. For some reason, most of the audience is wearing fur hats and coats, and under all that fur, I notice that all their faces seem the same. It's all face face fur fur fur face fur.... While we're up on the stage, in a great line-up—a Dixieland band starts playing "When the Saints Go Marching In" in the back of the house and comes tooting on down the aisles. All the furballs are clapping along.... Then all these little kids dressed in Mickey Mouse T-shirts come running out from the wings singing, in English, "Hands Across the Water." Then, all of a sudden a recording of "Long Tall Sally" by Little Richard comes blaring over the speakers, and all the kids start twisting and jitterbugging with us on stage while all the furry audience claps along. Then we are given flowers, and we all head out for the big opening-night banquet.

At the banquet, we are all sitting, eating old lox and old caviar, but, because of the prohibition, there's no vodka to wash it down. So I have my little bottles out and I'm pouring them under the table now, relaxed at last, feeling really at home in Russia, eating old lox and old caviar while I pour my Russian vodka under the table. The waiters are coming and going, singing. And all of a sudden, I hear this waiter behind me say in a deep Russian voice, "I saw that, Comrade."

What? Busted in Moscow for Smirnoff's? He takes it away from me. He's trying to show how well he reads English. It says "Smirnoff's, made in New Jersey." He's translating it, "Smirnoff's, made in New . . . polo shirt." He takes it away from me and keeps it as a souvenir.

But I'm feeling fine. And I'm relaxed at last, and quite zonked. And my translator, Misha, comes over to me and says, "Would you please speak tonight after the film *The Killing Fields*."

I say, "What?"

"The Killing Fields."

"I didn't know that was on the list of festival films. Well, sure I will say something. I don't know what I could add, or whatever, but I will go."

We arrive, the lights come up and, by God, people are standing up and asking open questions. I'm up there with Misha. The first man to stand up says, "Why here? Why this film, now, in Moscow, huh? Why you think?"

And I say, "Well . . . I would say that the parallels

between you guys and Cambodia is, uh—Afghanistan, of course! What do you think about Afghanistan? Why aren't you out in the streets protesting?"

As soon as I ask this question I can see the Russian film commissioner in the back of the house gesturing, "Cut! Cut! Cut!"

But the lights stayed up and so did the sound, and I thought, *glasnost* has arrived. More people started jumping up and yelling, "Afghanistan? We know nothing about Afghanistan. You read more in your paper than we read." And it turned into a very open, passionate, fiery question-and-answer session. I don't remember a lot of what was said, but I know it was passionate and open, and I thought it would have no repercussions. Until we got to Leningrad and the translation of *Swimming to Cambodia* suddenly disappeared.

We had sent the text over months ahead; it had been beautifully translated. They'd done a great job. You have to understand, none of the films had subtitles. It would have been too expensive. They all sent the text over to be translated ahead of time, and then they had one Russian reading all the roles. The sound was turned down low while the Russian read all the lines over a microphone. If you can imagine, *The Empire Strikes Back*—"*Ya prepodcheatayou potzyellovat* 'wookie' "[1]; *The Wizard of Oz*—"*Muy piedyom vidit bolshebnik*"[2]; *Children of a Lesser God* . . . ! But *Swimming to Cambodia* was really the least problematic because it was just one person speaking.

But now our translation was missing and no one

---

[1] "I prefer to kiss a wookie."
[2] "We're off to see the wizard."

seemed to know anything about it, which made me very paranoid. I was sure that its disappearance had something to do with my getting the audience to talk so openly about Afghanistan. Renée was more positive in her thinking and thought that our translator in Moscow had given it to some underground press in order to get it published. As for me, I went back to our hotel and lay down on the bed to talk to the chandelier, telling it, *Please, I'll never talk about Afghanistan again if you only slip our translation under the door,* but it never came. And I went to the Russian film commissioner and told him that we could not go on with the screenings of *Swimming* unless the translation was located, and he said, "Translation? We must call—bring him vodka—call Moscow, then—bring him caviar, bring . . . bring him flowers." The whole place was designed to make you feel like it's all your fault. It is the perfect place for a guilty person.

At last they decided to show the film with a translator who had never seen it, but who would translate it on the spot as he watched. I decided to go sit in the audience to see what would happen, because I was sure it was going to be a travesty.

So I'm sitting there in the audience and the film begins, and you hear me talking very low and very fast: "In 1984, I met this incredible British documentary filmmaker, Roland Joffe. A very intense man, a combination of Jesus, Zorro, and Rasputin—heart of Jesus, body of Zorro, eyes of Rasputin."

And then you hear, *"Njup nyub nyub neb juv lev."*
And I say, "Misha, Misha, what did he say?"

And Misha says, "An interesting director you met one time."

I said, "Stop! Stop the film, please!" People were walking out in droves, the place was a shambles, everyone was talking. "Stop! Misha, please tell them to stop. I want to get up and apologize."

And Misha says, "Do not go up there. They will throw fruits and vegetables at you."

Then I got up on stage and called the people back into the theater. Misha was shaking at my side and I said, "Come back in here, please. I hear you were going to throw fruits and vegetables at me if I came up here and I have to tell you I'm honored. I don't know where you were going to find them. And once you did, why you would waste them on me? But I have to say . . . Misha, are you translating this? This has been a very interesting and confusing time for me and I would like to try to redeem the evening, if possible, by taking questions from the house."

So Misha with a shaky hand passes out three-by-five cards for the audience to write their questions on. The first question to come up reads: "Why did Dustin Hoffman make *Tootsie?*"

And I said, "You're going to have to make these questions a little more personal."

The next question that comes up is: "What do you think of the following writers: Faulkner, Hesse, Thomas Mann, and Kafka?"

This is all one question and I assume they're serious and I said, "Well, as for Faulkner—I've only read one of his books, *The Sound and the Fury,* and I was totally satisfied. As for Hesse—way too romantic for me. I couldn't get past page seven of *Steppenwolf,* although I tried fourteen times. Uh, Thomas Mann I like very much. I just reread *The Magic Mountain* last year. Now as far as Kafka goes, I have to tell you people I've not paid a lot of attention to him. But since my trip here to Russia, I think I will read him with new insight."

They laughed, they thought that was funny.

Now the next question that comes up I was a little thrown by. I didn't know what they were talking about. It was very personal and kind of got my Achilles heel. It read, "Why are you so armored?"

Now the last thing I wanted to do was to appear armored in front of a Russian audience. I thought, maybe they're picking up on something here. I have been sitting behind a table for years, and I was sitting down on stage with Misha, and maybe that's what's giving that impression. Maybe they were picking up on all that table energy. I thought, maybe I should stand up and show the Russians my body. So I stand up. It's a cabaret situation. I'm a little stiff because, I have to tell you, it's quite cold there. There's a stand-up microphone and I bring it over. Misha comes over beside me. He's still shaking all over. He's never translated in front of a large audience before, he's only done it one-on-one. I myself would like to just get up and moonwalk, if I could, for the Russian audience —but, I don't know how to moonwalk—or do a body roll from the sixties with a little B. B. King music, you know. But there was no B. B. King music.

So instead, I talked. And I told the Russian audience a true story about how just that morning I got thrown out

56

of the Hermitage museum. We'd all voted that morning to go to the Hermitage and the bus was waiting outside. And we were all supposed to get on it at ten o'clock. Now, it's no easy job to get a bunch of American film actors on a bus at ten o'clock in the morning, particularly if it's being run by a communist who's not used to giving orders. When Renée and I were traveling in Nicaragua with American socialists, and the bus was supposed to leave at ten o'clock, there was no line to get on the bus. The bus simply filled up at ten o'clock in one big, simultaneous, earnest blob. If you weren't on the bus at ten o'clock, the bus left without you, and you stayed home and did penance. Now, when we were in Leningrad traveling, and the bus was supposed to leave at ten o'clock in the morning to go to the museum, Renée and I got on at ten o'clock. Ten-thirty, Carrie Fisher gets on. She looks around, she doesn't see anyone. She gets off and writes another chapter of her book. Daryl Hannah gets on the bus. Daryl Hannah doesn't see Carrie Fisher. Daryl Hannah gets off and searches for coffee with caffeine. Marlee Matlin gets on the bus. Marlee Matlin doesn't see Daryl Hannah, doesn't see Carrie Fisher. Marlee Matlin gets off and goes and practices her Russian sign language. Matt Dillon gets on the bus. Matt Dillon walks up and down and up and down the bus and gets off and goes and searches for vodka. Richard Gere gets on the bus. Richard Gere looks around, doesn't see Carrie Fisher, doesn't see Daryl Hannah, doesn't see Marlee Matlin, doesn't see Matt Dillon. Richard Gere gets off the bus and goes and writes a letter to the Dalai Lama. This leaves Renée and me in the back of the bus, taking notes.

At last, the bus is off, and by noon we reach the Hermitage. And we arrive with our cameras around our necks, and when the guards see our cameras they immediately say, "No, no. Nyet photo. No photo. No photograph, please." So we keep our cameras down. But one of the actresses is holding a video camera, by her left leg, that is on all the time. She would turn it on as soon as she got up in the morning and leave it running all day. For the entire trip, she is holding it by her left knee. It must be an experimental film of some sort—*Moscow From My Left Knee* kind of situation.

So we begin our tour through the Hermitage and always, when we're on these tours we end up in a "V" formation. Whoever has the most popular film at the time is right in the front, and we all line up behind. It happened to be Richard Gere. We looked like Canadian geese flying south.

And around the corner comes another "V" formation of American high school students from Westchester who are going around the world on a school trip. And they've stopped in Odessa, and they've put the trip on hold and come down to Leningrad to see the Hermitage museum. They round the corner in a "V" formation with all their cameras around their necks. They see us. They go, "Holy shit! It's Daryl Hannah. I know it's Daryl Hannah and oh my God! It's Matt Dillon! Whoo! It's Richard Gere! Wow!" Flash! Flash! Flash! And they all begin madly to take photos of us.

And the museum guards are running everywhere crying, "Nyet! No photo! No. Nyet! Nyet! Nyet photo! No photograph!"

Why are Americans taking pictures of Americans?!!

58

Meanwhile, I'm over in the corner, because I've been recognized by some of the students. I've been recognized —thank God I've been recognized—for being on the David Letterman show. They are over there asking me, "What is David Letterman really like?"

And I would tell them, but I'm too hot. I've got my Chinese long silk underwear on, because it's so cold outside, and inside it's so hot in the museum. I can't get the balance. And I'm over there saying, "David Letterman? Oh, he's all right. I'd have to say that he's— you know, he treated me fine. He treated me like a downtown artist. He seemed happy to have me on the show. Maybe . . . maybe if I was a woman it would have been different."

All the time I'm talking to the students about David Letterman, I'm also rolling my pants up to my knee to try to cool off my legs. I'm standing there with my pants rolled up so that now the bottom of my Chinese long silk underwear is showing a pure white. And I'm not really thinking about it. All I know is that I'm cooling off. If I had thought about it, I guess I would have said I looked like a Bowery bum or a Maine clam digger, but I didn't care because I was cool at last. All of a sudden, behind me, these great matronly museum guards grab me under my arms and start to throw me out of the Hermitage. I cry out, "Misha, Misha! Come quickly! Translate! Why are they throwing me out of the Hermitage?"

Misha comes over, translates and says, "For imitating royalty."

I told this to the Russian audience and they said, "This could be true."

———

59

The following day, something awful happened—Renée came down with a wicked flu. I'm afraid she caught it in the Moscow baths. She had gone to the baths in Moscow. They were fantastic, great old steam baths. But many Muscovites had the flu and they were trying to purge themselves of the flu in the baths by strapping themselves with birch leaves. And they were letting go of what they called a "sick juice," which was flying off of these birch leaves. The "sick juice" hit Renée in the face and did her in and she had a major fever.

She was burning up. She thought she'd come to die in Russia—her people were from Russia and she thought she'd come home at last to die there.

I sat by the bed like a Christian Science practitioner. I didn't know what to do. What do you do? How do you get a doctor in America, let alone Russia? Yet I tried and they didn't understand my English or the translation. Renée was too sick to talk.

I thought, "I will call a hotel doctor. There must be a hotel doctor." And they mistranslated my request and sent up the kitchen health inspector instead. Then, after that, they sent up a doctor who had a huge needle rolled in butcher paper—when I asked him if it was a disposable needle he said, "Did you bring your own?"

He was very offended. He shot Renée up and her fever went down a little. Then they sent another doctor to try to impress us. In comes this great matron with a babushka and gold teeth. She comes in with no implements at all, walks over, tells Renée to open her mouth. She grabs the table lamp next to Renée, holds it over Renée's throat, takes the teaspoon from the teacup and holds her tongue down, and says, "You'll live," and leaves.

So I say, "Renée, listen, your fever's going down. Please try to eat something. I just saw some green vegetables— the first I've seen since we've been in Leningrad. You've got to have them. They're canned green peas, I think. And they're under . . . well, I don't know if you want to eat what they're under. I don't know what it is. If you take a boomerang, an Australian boomerang, and glue chicken meat to it, that's what it looked like. Like Boomerang Chicken. Or Wing of Odd Bird. So order the Boomerang Chicken, but just eat the peas." I drag Renée out of bed. I get her down there. But by the time we get down there they've run out of green peas and they've replaced them instead with forty hot green olives.

Renée just pleads, "Spald, let's get out of here before what happened to them happens to us."

That propelled us out of Russia. We were able to escape just in time. Renée was so happy to get out and not be hospitalized. We arrive in Helsinki which had seemed like this gray Nordic city on the way through. Now it was like an Easter egg. Suddenly there was all this color. All the children wore pastel snowsuits. And there was food! Real food!

We get back to New York City. We get back to that island off the coast of America, Manhattan. And I am so happy to be back. I am cured from all that Russian common unhappiness. I am so happy to be back in the land of freedom of speech, freedom of the press, that I bow down and kiss the Monster. I feel honored to be able to work on my book now and I'm almost finished. Brewster has almost made it to Bali.

He's made it to Sydney, Australia. And he's trapped there. He can't quite make it to Bali because the two Australian airlines, Ansett and Qantas, are on strike. He won't fly on the Balinese airline, Garuda, because he won't fly on any airline where the pilots believe in reincarnation. So he's trapped on Bondi Beach. And I mean really trapped. He can't even go in swimming. He can't go in swimming because since he's been in Australia he's been eating a fish called filet, which he finds out is a euphemism for shark. Now he won't go in the water because he thinks the brothers and the sisters are going to take revenge.

The other thing that's driving him nuts is that he is surrounded on the beach by all these beautiful bare-breasted Australian women. And he can't get near them, because he's on a mission—remember, he wants to get to Bali. He's trying to be loyal to his girlfriend, Cleo, and also, don't forget, he is traveling with his mother's money. So he's getting so turned on by these women that he can't bear it. He's trying to push his libido down. And you can't keep that stuff down.

He gets back to the hotel and he's trying to relieve himself with these ornate masturbation rituals, in which he's now shaved all his pubic hair to try to get in touch with some younger version of himself. He's right-handed and he's working a lot with his left hand to try to surprise himself. He's having a wild time with a Hoover vacuum cleaner, but the sound of it is so distracting that he's

62

wrapped it in a blanket and put it in the closet, and has run the hose out under the door.

And I've just taken that section in to my typist, a spinster from Queens who lives with her sister on West 48th Street. Every time I go in to see her, I'm always looking over to see what she thinks of the book, because she's the only one who's read it. But she never gives an inch. She acts totally professional, gets up and moves like a great tortoise to the kitchen table, where she lights up a Virginia Slim and hands me my bill. I get out a check, sign it with my Pilot pen, and give it to her.

This time, I come in, pick up *this* new section of writing, look it over, try to catch her eye. But she doesn't look back. She just gets up and moves like a great tortoise, lights her Virginia Slim, then looks over at me and says, "Well, Mr. Gray. You're definitely a writer. But I hope this is fiction . . . or you're in *real* trouble."

She threw me out of the Garden of Eden! She judged the book. I wish she'd never said anything! All of a sudden I think, oh my God, how—with the world coming to an end, people starving, the ozone layer ripping, and the tropical rain forests disappearing at a football field a second—how can I be writing this solipsistic, narcissistic, self-indulgent pile of poop? I mean, the best thing I could do is take it up to the Brooklyn Bridge and toss it off at dawn. But I had to finish it first. I had to finish it, read through it, and then judge it.

I should have unplugged the phone. Just as I'm about to get Brewster to Bali, the phone rings and it's Gregory Mosher, the director of Lincoln Center Theater, saying,

"Hi, Gregory here. Listen, Spalding, how would you like to be the stage manager of the eighties? How would you like to play the Stage Manager in Thornton Wilder's *Our Town* on Broadway?"

I can't believe what I'm hearing and I say, "Gregory, listen, thank you very much. I am honored, but I can't. I have to finish my book."

And he says, "Write it in the morning. We'll rehearse in the afternoon."

I say, "Gregory, it's not just the book. I would come and see the play, I love the play. It's a favorite of mine, but I, I don't think I could do it. I simply don't think I could say those lines. They're too wholesome and folksy. Get Garrison Keillor."

"We don't want Garrison Keillor, we want you. This is a farewell to all the sentimental *Our Town*s. It's a farewell to the Hallmark card of *Our Town*. We want you. We want your dark, New England, ironic sensibility."

"Well, Gregory, you got me there. I'll tell you what. Give me a day to think about it."

I hang up. I think, my God! This is the chance of a lifetime. Here it is. It's a limited run. I could work on the Monster in my dressing room. The role is great. I could speak from my heart at last, provided I could memorize the lines—and I could at last use my New England accent. So I think I'd better just call my Hollywood agent, see if she has any opinions on this before I say yes or no.

I call her up and she says, "Dear heart, dear heart! No way! Why, after all these years of acting, would you want to be a stage manager?"

———

So I say yes, and trumpets blow! And they announce it in *The New York Times* Friday section: "At last we've found a stage manager for the eighties."

And I can't wait to get to rehearsal. I love the whole cast of twenty-eight. I jump up, I run down to the Canal Street subway station. I run past the guy sucking the tokens out of the turnstile. I ride up on the number one train, buying yet another copy of the same issue of *Street News,* feeling so fortunate. I get out of the number one train. I jump over the exploding gas mains, make my way through the popping water pipes, step over the homeless, push past the crack dealers on the back steps of the Lyceum Theater, and I'm in Grover's Corners, New Hampshire! And everyone's singing, smiling and happy in period costumes—oh, it's just fantastic!

Opening night is a to-die evening. I mean Penelope Ann Miller's delivery of Emily's farewell cemetery speech to the earth is so heart wrenching, so beautiful, that I'm crying. And as I pull the curtain closed at the end of the play—I'm not acting—I'm crying.

As I go off to the big opening night party at Sardi's I can't help feeling that I've completed something big in my life—and like any actor, I'm fantasizing about what the press might say about me. Things like: "This once traditional actor who deserted us for the underground has returned with an ingenious interpretation of the Stage Manager in Thornton Wilder's *Our Town.* . . . He has that special something that translates Grover's Corners into contemporary America." I couldn't sleep, thinking about what the critics would say. And in the morning I ran out and bought all the papers and dumped them in Renée's lap, and said, "Renée, just read the good parts. I'm going to go brush my teeth. Just shout out a couple of good lines, I'll read the rest later."

From the bathroom I hear her cry, "Oh my God, Spald. Wait, let me look at the *Post*. . . . Oooh! Ooohh! Let me look at the *Times*. . . . Oh, Spald, no, don't come in here."

It was unanimous. All the critics agreed. I had destroyed Thornton Wilder. They wanted to tar and feather me and run me out of town. The *Daily News* said, "This just goes to prove avant-garde actors can't act. Spalding Gray couldn't even maintain a New England accent." Edith Oliver of *The New Yorker,* good old Edith —I had to get out a dictionary to understand her review. Edith Oliver's review read, "Spalding Gray's deportment was a blight to the town." I pictured myself like walking Dutch elm disease coming down Main Street. But Clive Barnes of the *Post* said it all. Clive Barnes said, "Spalding Gray came from outer space and Gregory Mosher left him there."

So I come to the theater the following night and oh my God I'm down. But the cast are all whistling and singing in their period costumes and asking, "What's wrong, Spald?"

"You know what's wrong. You read the reviews."

"No, we never read the reviews."

"What?"

"No, actors never read their reviews. Maybe you read yours because you're a writer."

I say, "Stop it. You never read the reviews?"

"No. Why empower those assholes? If you want to read reviews, read them at the end of the run. Don't read them during a run. What if a critic says you said a line in a particular way? You'll never be able to say that line fresh again. You'll hear that critic's voice in your head every time you speak the line."

Oh, how that did happen to me! Frank Rich of *The New York Times* said that I was "snide, flip, and condescending to the audience as well as the people in the town," and I know that I wasn't. I know it. But Frank wrote it in *The New York Times,* therefore I must've been. He picked out a line from the beginning of the play where he felt I was the most flip and condescending. The line simply reads, "Nice town, y'know what I mean?"

So, I come in the night after the reviews, I walk on stage . . . Look, I thought the audience was going to throw fruits and vegetables at me. Then I realize they're a wonderful New York audience and, like all New York audiences, are waiting to judge for themselves. So I come out and . . . have you seen *Our Town?* Do you know the play? The stage is empty and I have to describe everything in the town: all of the churches and stores and I begin with the churches and Grover's Corners has every church but a mosque, a Christian Science church and a synagogue. First I show the church where the young couple in the play, Emily and George, get married. Then I describe the Main Street of the town: Here's the soda fountain where Emily and George first fall in love. George's family lives here—Doc Gibbs, the town doctor, is his father. And right next door are Emily Webb and her family. And I say, "And this is Mrs. Webb's garden. Just like Mrs. Gibbs', only it's got a lot of sunflowers, too. Right here . . . 's a big butternut tree." And then I say it.

"Nice town, y'know what I mean?"

And it just comes out of me with this big shit-eating grin, and for a moment I feel totally awkward and self-conscious, but I get through it all right and on to the rest of the play. Much to my surprise, I find that I love doing the play because I'm able to get in touch with Thornton Wilder's language; because of it, I'm able to transcend everything the critics wrote. I get swept back to New England where I came from. I get swept back to New England where I used to believe in God and eternity and all the things the play is about. Before I came to New York City and became a hardcore Freudian existentialist. And now, all of a sudden, Wilder was softening me up again. It was beautiful to speak those lines about eternity and I began to think a lot about the Tibetan monks. They spend their lifetime visualizing their afterlife until they create one so strongly in their imagination that when they die, they slip right into that place. I was beginning to see that play as a kind of New England Tibetan Book of the Dead. I would speak about eternity eight shows a week. I thought, if I really believed it as I said it, maybe I would get there.

But the cemetery scene was the most powerful for me. You see, Emily dies in childbirth and her funeral takes place on stage in the third act. I had never been to a funeral before. Not even my mother's, because I was in Mexico trying to take a vacation when all of that happened. And now here I was going to a funeral—Emily's funeral—eight shows a week and this was giving me a sense of closure around the issue of having missed my mother's funeral. Eight shows a week Emily is brought out on stage all huddled in and hidden amongst the mourners all dressed in black with their umbrellas held over their heads, and they begin to sing Emily's favorite hymn. It's very beautiful. I'm standing there against the bare back wall of the stage just watching. The mourners exit, leaving Emily dressed in a simple white dress. She walks across the stage to sit in the straight-backed chair that represents her grave. And she sits down amongst all the other recent dead who are all sitting bolt upright, staring up at the stars above. Everyone is so peacefully concentrated. It's all so beautiful. Franny Conroy, who is playing Mother Gibbs, is sitting in the front row. She has been doing transcendental meditation for the past fifteen years and she's in a deep trance.

The little boy playing Emily's brother, Wally Webb, is an eleven-year-old boy, and he is sitting there, as well, not blinking for forty minutes while I talk about eternity. Try to imagine the dead, motionless in their graves on a high windy hilltop in New Hampshire, the wind blowing through elm trees, a dark rain falling, a kind of quiet sadness on their faces as they gradually grow more distant from their lives on earth. But a part of them stays there before they vanish forever. The part that is expectant, hopeful. And in the play, I say: "And they stay here while the earth part of them burns away, burns out. . . . They're waitin' for something they feel is comin'. Something important, and great. Aren't they waitin' for the eternal part in them to come out clear?"

And every night I would perform this and every night it would basically be the same. Except often, when you do a long run of a play you have what I call a unifying accident, in which something so strange happens in the play, that it suddenly unites the audience in the realization that we are all here together at this one moment in time. It's not television. It's not the movies. And it probably won't be repeated the following night. It happened as I was speaking of the dead and I say, "And they stay here while the earth part of them burns away, burns out. . . . They're waitin' for something they feel is comin'. Something important and great. . . ." As I say this, I turn and gesture to them, waiting, and, just as I turn and gesture, the little eleven-year-old boy playing Wally Webb projectile vomits! Like a hydrant it comes, hitting some of the dead on their shoulders! The other dead levitate out of their chairs, in total shock, around him and drop back down. Franny Conroy, deep in her meditative trance, is slowly wondering, "Why is it raining on stage?" The little boy flees from his chair, vomit pouring from his mouth. Splatter. Splatter. Splatter. I'm standing there. My knees are shaking. The chair is empty. The audience is thunderstruck! There is not a sound coming from them, except for one little ten-year-old boy in the eighth row. He *knows* what he saw. . . . He is laughing!

At this point, I don't know whether to be loyal to Thornton Wilder and go on with the next line as written, or attempt what might be one of the most creative improvs in the history of American theater. At last I decide to be loyal to Wilder and simply go on with the next line, and I turn to the empty chair and say: "Aren't they waitin' for the eternal part in them to come out clear?"

Then, after three months, I finished the run of the play and I went upstairs to my dressing room to pack up my Monster. I had come to the end of the book, and the character has at last made it to Bali and he's lying there under the stars, remembering that first vacation he tried to take in Mexico, and how, when he came home, all he found left of his mother was ashes in an urn, in a box, by his father's bed. And he's lying there under the stars, thinking maybe he should try to write a short story about how he feels about that. But looking up at the stars, he suddenly feels so peaceful, so present, he thinks maybe he should skip the story and try to take a vacation instead.

Thank you for coming and good night.

Other *Others*

Not everyone I interviewed on the Mark Taper Forum
stage in Los Angeles was as weird as I make them out to
be in the monologue. To some extent I understand now
how I was taking an easy shot at their idiosyncrasies. But,
on the other hand, their odd stories make for good
drama.

When I originally set out to do the project, I had the
intention of interviewing more refugees and first-
generation Americans, particularly focusing on the
Cambodian community in Long Beach. But I found that
community to be one of the most private and difficult to
infiltrate, even with my recognition from *The Killing
Fields*. I did at last get to interview one Cambodian man
and two Cambodian women. But in all three cases, their
stories were very protected, politic, and cautious. It was
naive of me to think that they could easily open up to the
public after what they had been through. To cover up

their past history had become a necessary act for survival. Now they were just happy to be in America. Try as I did, I could never get them to tell me one thing they didn't like about living in Los Angeles. They were all extremely sweet, humble, and thankful just to be alive.

After much pushing, I do remember at last squeezing one comment of dissatisfaction out of one of the Cambodian women. I think it was a simple complaint about the aggressive way in which people drive in L.A. After the interview was over she came up to me and pleaded with me to strike all her negative comments from the record. She approached me in such a state of frantic desperation that I immediately promised her never to use any of our taped conversation. The level of fear and distress that emanated from her gave me yet another insight into the still-lingering horrors of the Pol Pot regime.

As for the woman who told me her story of being picked up by a mother spaceship on the Ventura freeway (one night in performance I accidentally referred to the Ventura freeway as "the Ventura Spaceway" and have left it in the transcription of the monologue), she had actually begun by telling me what I took to be a more plausible, and therefore more interesting story, about how she enjoys testing herself by going out alone into the desert to camp. She opened the interview by telling me a vivid story of how she spent one Thanksgiving night in a cave filled with bats, stalagmites, and stalactites, sleeping alone on a blanket and eating only a cold can of Dinty Moore stew for dinner. I found this story to be fascinating, but when I pressed her further, she cut me off by saying, "Aren't you going to ask me about what I came here to talk about?" At that point I saw that she was not comfortable talking about anything but spaceships, so I took that as my cue to ask her about "the mother spaceship"—an incident we had discussed briefly on the phone when I was screening her for the interview. The spaceship incident was much more fuzzy and fantastical, more like a comic-book description than a real-life diary entry. It lacked the detail her cave story had and for me the "truth" is always in the details.

There were many other interesting people I interviewed but did not have room for in the monologue. There was a wonderful man who happened to be gay and had been in a relationship with the same man, who had come to the theater with him and was sitting in the audience, for thirty years. He told a magnificent story about the time he and his lover set out one day with all their savings to purchase their dream car—a Rolls-Royce. On the way to the Rolls dealer they decided instead to take the money and adopt two children. They adopted two boys and raised them to be wonderful men, and, as he said, with a wry smile and a wink, "They both turned out to be straight. I don't know where we went wrong."

Years later now, other people I interviewed still come to mind, leaving vivid memory traces that will stay with me for a lifetime. Betty Clarke, head of the Los Angeles Braille Institute and blind herself, comes to mind. I chose her because I wanted to get a blind person's perspective on L.A. Betty is an extraordinarily up person. Her total lack of self-pity put me to shame and made me get some perspective on my L.A. *mishigas*. She told me a story about using a white cane for the first time in L.A.:

But I think I'm lucky. I really sometimes think I wouldn't want my life to have been any different because I meet such neat people, and wonderful people. I do not like a white cane, but the time came. I was going to Europe [Betty loves to travel] and I thought, well, I better prepare myself, in case I have to be alone over there. So I took mobility orientation lessons. And my teacher said, "I will meet you down at the Braille Institute," and for that I have to take two buses. "Get one at Marshall, and get one at Fountain and Vermont." And I had everything and I had done it a thousand times. So he called and said, "I'm here, and I'll meet you when you get here and you're on your own." So I started out, and, at the corner of Griffith and Mona was a big mud puddle, and I stepped in and both feet went up and I went "plop" on my you-know-what, and I was mud from one end to the other. Then, before I knew what was happening, here were two marvelous men, wiping me off, saying, "Are you all right?" So I made two great friends there. So then I walked down to the corner and got on the bus and everybody on the bus said, "What happened to *you*?" Well, by the time I got to Vermont and Fountain, I was friends with everybody on that bus and the bus driver was so super. When I got off the bus he said, "Now I don't want you walking across Vermont by yourself." So he said, "I will drive the bus across and you walk along the side of the bus and that way I'll protect you with my bus!" So I do it. I walk across Vermont and he's driving across Vermont, and all the time we are just having this great conversation 'cause he's left his door open. Then when we got to the other side of Vermont, he honked his horn at the other bus that was at the bus stop and he told the other driver to wait for me. Oh, it was just marvelous. So I had a great time and I think that when you do have a visual or any kind of physical problem, it's not so bad actually because you get to know so many nice people. For instance, I would never have met you!

Last of all, Raymond Hirai will be forever memorable. In fact, Raymond seems almost like a fictional character to me now. Before interviewing him, I visited him at his home, which was one room in a very pristine flophouse in what, in some more romantic times in America, might have been called Skid Row. It was in downtown L.A. and Raymond lived on the only lively block in all of Los Angeles. It was so lively that it looked like the cover of some R. Crumb comic book come alive. It was as though all the people on a Sunday in New York City's Washington Square Park had blown in on a tornado and were all contained in that one block. It was the only great street scene I'd ever witnessed in Los Angeles and it was jumpin'! There were crack dealers dealing openly. There were wild tribes of homeless living in huge converted refrigerator cartons, with little windows cut into the sides, like the ones we used to play in when we were kids.

There were mixed groups of men and women all hanging out on broken benches sipping quarts of Colt 45 and Ripple wine. There was one very tall black guy with a ghetto blaster rap rap rapping away while he went through some of the fastest and most beautifully choreographed jump rope moves I have ever seen. My assistant had somehow procured Raymond's address and I was making my way through that jumble of a jungle to get to Raymond's front door.

Inside, Raymond received me graciously. The room he lived in was about sixteen feet by twenty feet. There was a narrow bed, a straight-backed chair, one barred window, and a little hot-plate in the corner where he prepared all his meals. Raymond was, he said, ninety-eight years old. He was a very thin little Japanese man who weighed about as much as he was old. He sat on his bed and I sat in the straight-backed chair while he told me some of his story. Usually I don't like to know too much about the people I'm going to interview on stage. I'd rather get to know them in front of the audience. But with Raymond, I couldn't resist.

He told me that his family moved from Japan to Utah, to a town called Sandy, when he was only four years old. Shortly after that they moved to Los Angeles and he has been living in the same neighborhood ever since. He used to live across the street from the place he lives in now but they tore the building down. So he has lived on the same street for about eighty years. Over the years he held a number of odd jobs, including extra work in films. He was, he told me, the only Japanese extra in the film version of Pearl S. Buck's *The Good Earth,* all the rest were Chinese. And it was he who had the idea of how to create the plague of locusts in the film. When the special-effects people couldn't figure out how to create that great dark cloud of locusts falling upon the fields, Raymond suggested that they dye tons of popcorn black and dump it out of airplanes. They took his suggestion and it worked.

Raymond told me he was friends with Charlie Chaplin, having met him through Chaplin's Japanese gardener. Also, he was good friends with William Holden, who had once brought him one of the first sex dolls from Japan. At this point he got up and opened his closet door to show me. He opened the door and there it was, a deflated life-size Japanese sex doll hanging on a coat hanger. "You fill her up with warm water and take her to bed. Very warm. Very good pussy," Raymond said with a wink to me.

Returning to his bed, Raymond pulled out a gold-colored fishing net from underneath and told me he had made it while he was a prisoner of war in a Japanese internment camp that had been set up in the Santa Anita racetrack. He told me his aunt had died in the camp but he had survived and thrived because he had been put in charge of entertainment. Now he spends a lot of time at Santa Anita. In fact, all he has done for years is play the horses, going from track to track. When Santa Anita is closed he goes to Pomona or Del Mar and wins as much as he wants, and the following day he goes out and loses because, as he told me, his friends who win all the time end up dying and he plans to live to be one hundred and seventeen years old because he just keeps turning the money around. When I asked him how he could be such a steady winner he told me that he goes down to the paddock and looks the horses in the eye just before the race and he can tell just like that which horse will be a winner that day. The following day, when he goes to lose his money, he looks for a bloodshot eye and puts all his money down on that horse, saving just enough for groceries. Then he undid his pants and took them down to reveal a second set of trousers underneath. Out of the pocket he pulled a roll of money that would choke a racehorse. I could not believe my eyes. There must have been more than three thousand dollars there, and all the time I had been wondering how much money I should be paying him for the interview. "But aren't you afraid someone will mug you on the street?" I asked incredulously, not taking into consideration that it wouldn't have mattered where the money really ended up. "No problem," Raymond said. "I know karate. Just break wrist like that. One chop," as he chopped at the air with one, two, three clear strokes.

Then I asked him what he'd been reading lately and he said, *California Raw*, which I thought at first was some sort of new comic book I hadn't heard of. Then I figured out that he was saying "California law." And there it was, sitting in the corner right next to his hot-plate, a huge book containing all the laws of California. He was reading it cover to cover. He told me that it all started out with his wanting to assist a friend with his alimony problems; he ended up reading the entire book because he always reads a book from start to finish. Then he tells me the last book he read was a fourteen-hundred-page book on mineralogy. Then he gets up and gets out his mineral collection from under the bed, and it seems to me at this point he has a whole little world stored under there. We sit and look at minerals for a while. After looking at these various beautifully colored minerals, our conversation winds toward women, and I want to know if the inflatable sex doll is his only girlfriend, and he tells me no. He has a number of girlfriends and he refers to them all by number. He begins talking about Number Eight. In fact he tells me that he was just with Number Eight last night and she's about thirty-five years old and very pretty, a good cook and doesn't mind being referred to as Number Eight. I ask him what they do together besides making love, which he claims he still does often, and he says, "We play cards and then I read her future in her fingernails."

"You read her fingernails?" I ask, mildly confused but open to just about anything at this point. And he goes on to tell me about how we all have four million red blood cells and nine million white blood cells and you can tell when that ratio is out of line by what's going on in your fingernails.

We have a lovely day together and the only thing we don't do is go to Santa Anita, which is still a big regret for me to this day.

When I finally got Raymond on stage to interview him, we ended up going over a lot of the same material we covered in his room, which was not perhaps as fresh as it could have been had I not visited him first. But what we did do on stage that for me was quite remarkable, was to re-create a street attack that had recently been perpetrated on him. Some guy had tried to mug Raymond and he had broken the man's wrist. We both stood up on the stage and I, armed with a Pilot pen to simulate a knife, went after Raymond. I was amazed to feel the energy that came out of his arm as he grabbed me and twisted me onto the floor with such speed and agile strength that I, for a moment, did not know what had hit me.

Toward the end of the interview I asked him if he had ever been married, and, when he said no, I asked why not. He said, "Well, I don't know why, but you know, I look so bad, and not real good looking, and I have no head. I'm just a nobody and a dummy but I don't know why, there's so many women come up to me so I can't stay with only one woman. That's the only reason I don't get married. But very strange things happen lately. Two women claim I'm their father. They call me father and they come over and clean my room and make my bed twice or three times a week. They said their mother told them I am their father and they don't look so old and they call me father and they act like a daughter and keep things nice so I don't mind."

Then I ended the interview as I often do by asking him if he had any questions he wanted to ask me. He answered by saying, "Yeah, I don't know why you hire a guy like me. I'm no good for nothing, can't help you with nothing, only thing I can tell you is your palm says you are making a great success in early future." And Raymond gently took my left hand and pointed to a confluence of lines that created a star-shaped asterisk I had never noticed before, right in the center of my left palm.

About the Author

Born in Providence, Rhode Island, in 1941, writer, actor, and performer Spalding Gray has created a series of thirteen monologues that have been performed throughout the United States, Europe, and Australia, including *Sex and Death to the Age 14, Swimming to Cambodia,* and *Terrors of Pleasure.* His *Monster in a Box* and *Swimming to Cambodia* have both been made into feature films, and *Terrors of Pleasure* was televised for HBO. With the Wooster Group, which he cofounded in 1977, Mr. Gray wrote and performed the autobiographical trilogy *Three Places in Rhode Island.* His films include *The Killing Fields, Swimming to Cambodia, True Stories, Stars and Bars, Clara's Heart, Beaches,* and *The Image* for HBO. His publications include a collection of monologues entitled *Sex and Death to the Age 14, Swimming to Cambodia,* and the novel *Impossible Vacation,* to be published by Alfred A. Knopf. Mr. Gray has received a Guggenheim Fellowship and grants from the National Endowment for the Arts and the Rockefeller Foundation.

ALSO AVAILABLE FROM
VINTAGE BOOKS

Sex and Death to the Age 14
by Spalding Gray

Spalding Gray's first collection of monologues "inspires a reaction rare in theatre: affection. You're aware of the art involved, but most of the time it might be you and he in a bar somewhere, two friends from way, way back"(*Los Angeles Times*).

"A sit-down monologuist with the soul of a stand-up comedian... a contemporary Gulliver."

—*The New York Times*

"Gray burrows under the apparent homogeneity of American life to reveal marvels and curiosities as astonishing as any Alice encountered in Wonderland. His vision, as entertaining as it is idiosyncratic, has the effect of renewing yours."

—*Washington Post*

0-394-74257-5/$6.95

VINTAGE 🌣 BOOKS

AVAILABLE AT YOUR LOCAL BOOKSTORE, OR CALL TOLL-FREE
TO ORDER: 1-800-733-3000 (CREDIT CARDS ONLY). PRICES
SUBJECT TO CHANGE.